Professor Angelicus Visits
The Big Blue Ball

Professor Angelicus Visits
The Big Blue Ball

By
L. B. B. Ward

Illustrations By Coulter Watt

MumbleFish Books

Ward, L. B. B.
Professor Angelicus Visits the Big Blue Ball

Summary: When Zak and Ivy head to the river for the first day of fishing,
they have no idea they're going to find that the simplest act of kindness
toward the most improbable stranger will lead themselves and Zak's little
dog, Ziggy, on an incredible voyage to the farthest reaches of, above,
under, and, finally, far beyond the earth.

ISBN 0-9759649-0-9

Author Photograph © David Gilleece

Printed in USA
On Acid Free, 30% Post Consumer Recycled Paper
by George H Buchanan Co.

First Edition, February 2005
LCCN - 2004113205
MumbleFishbooks.com
(866) MUMBLES

This book is dedicated to the men in my life:

My father, Anthony Bressi,
My husband, Palmer Ward,
My son, Todd Blackburn,
My grandson, Zachary Blackburn

Special thanks to my good friend, Joe Hoey

This book would not exist without them all . . .

THE CHAPTERS

PROFESSOR ANGELICUS VISITS
THE BIG BLUE BALL

THE CREEK PATH
AND THE RIVER

It was the first day of spring, and it was Saturday. Zak didn't have to go to school. From his bedroom window he could see two robins poking at the wet spring grass. The trees were beginning to bud and he couldn't get dressed fast enough! This was the perfect day to head down to the river and go fishing.

Zak lived with his mom and dad and little dog, Ziggy, in a small stone house surrounded by cornfields on top of a hill.

Zak had gone fishing with his dad as far back as he could remember. But his dad had to work today, so Zak and Ziggy were going without him. They would follow the creek that ran by the house down to the river, where they were going to meet his friend, Ivy, at the boat rental office.

"Come on, Ziggy, let's get goin'," Zak called to the small

white and black dog as he ran to the garage for his fishing rod.

His father already had his carpenter's belt on and was climbing into his truck. "See ya, pal," he said. "Wish I was goin' with you—good luck."

"Thanks, Dad," said the boy.

"Wait a minute, Zak," called his mother from the kitchen window, "you almost forgot your lunch!"

"Oh! Thanks, Mom," said the dark-haired boy. He stuffed the lunch bag into his knapsack.

"And remember," she continued, "we're having dinner at six o'clock, so don't be late."

The path by the creek was rocky and wet, so Zak stepped carefully, with Ziggy staying close by his heels. The water was raging high from an early spring thaw, and small scattered patches of soft white snow were melting into the new green life that was waking up beneath his feet.

Zak had been here so many times he almost knew the creek bank by heart. He and Ivy would dig for arrowheads and pretend they were the Indians who had camped here hundreds of years before. They'd look for snakes and box turtles, and catch frogs. Last fall they had collected leaves for a fourth-grade school project.

As Zak walked along he could hear the birds singing while they were busy building their nests. He was pushing his way through the overgrown path when something moved in the brush. Suddenly, a young doe was looking him straight in the eye. Zak stopped in his tracks. Ziggy put his head flat to the ground and, with his behind sticking straight in the air, gave out a loud "Yelp!"

Frightened, the deer ran off so fast her feet barely touched the ground. Ziggy took off after her.

"Ziggy! Come back here!" yelled Zak, running as fast as he could, trying to keep up. But the little dog disappeared into the woods. Finally Zak stopped and, catching his breath, sat down on a rock. He knew Ziggy would come back when he got tired, so he'd just sit and wait.

A branch snapped off a sycamore tree and fell to the ground. A crow called out from the top of a giant ash. Zak looked up at the huge old tree and wished he could grow that tall. He wondered how it would feel to have branches instead of arms and reach up and touch the deep blue sky.

A few minutes passed and Ziggy came racing back out of the brush, panting and wagging his tail. His shaggy fur was all covered with stickers and twigs.

Zak jumped up and, shaking his finger, said to the little dog, "You're a bad boy! You just had a bath and look at you now. You're all dirty again!"

Ziggy knew he had done something wrong. He dropped his tail between his legs and sat down.

Zak brushed Ziggy off, hoping there weren't any deer ticks on him. He knew that when the ground thawed, a tiny tick, no bigger than a freckle, could bite him and make him sick. Ziggy put his paw on Zak's knee. Zak patted him on the head, picked up his fishing rod, and the two of them continued down the path.

They passed the big gray barn and the old gristmill. They saw a beaver working on his dam. A red squirrel raced up a tree, and a field mouse scurried by their feet. They watched a rabbit nibble on some golden yellow crocuses that had pushed their way up through a tiny patch of snow.

The creek became much wider when it was merrily met by a smaller stream that tumbled and bubbled down from the hill. The woods grew thinner and, in the near distance, Zak could see the sunlight dancing on a giant waterfall that poured off the aqueduct of the old canal. Soon he'd be at the river.

* * *

The sun was beginning to burn off the morning mist that hung over the river like a gentle white veil. The water murmured and sparkled as it flowed along. Up in the sky the turkey buzzards that nested in the nearby cliffs were circling and gliding through the crisp spring air. Zak stood there by the river's edge and took a deep breath. He loved the smell of the river.

A fish jumped and Ziggy ran into the water, trying to catch it.

"Come back here, Ziggy," Zak said. "Let's go find Ivy. The shad are running!"

Zak and Ziggy headed toward the boat rental office, looking for Ivy. The small shed stood a few yards back from the water's edge. It was painted blue and white. Stacked all around it were canoes and small rowboats. Ivy was nowhere in sight, but two old fishermen from the city were there, renting a boat for the day.

Zak sat down on the stump of an old tree to wait for his friend. He couldn't help but overhear the old men talking as they loaded their gear into the boat.

"I sure hope we catch some fish today," said the taller man. He had white hair and the bluest eyes Zak had ever seen. "I've been coming here since I was a boy and there used to be an awful lot of fish in this river. When the shad were runnin', the fishermen would throw out their nets and catch thousands of 'em."

His friend raised his bushy eyebrows. Zak could see the lines furrowing his forehead.

"Thousands? Geez! I didn't realize. What happened to 'em all?" he asked.

"Too much commercial fishin', I guess," answered the tall man. "And the water got so dirty, the shad would die before they could make it up the river to spawn. One year they didn't catch a single fish. Of course now they've been cleanin' the river up. The shad are comin' back." He stopped and scratched his head. "But I don't know. This water looks awful low for this time of year. I wonder if it has anything to do with that pump they built."

"What pump?"

"It's just downstream a little ways. Once we get out in the channel, you'll see it. It pumps the water out of the river," he said.

"Why would they wanna do that—pump the water outta the river?" his friend asked.

"Who knows? Maybe for all the new houses they keep building. But I'll tell ya, the people around here sure didn't like it. I'm surprised you don't remember it. It was on TV and everything! They just stood there on that site and wouldn't move. They blocked the bulldozers and tried to stop the guys with the chainsaws from cuttin' down the trees. Finally the cops came and dragged 'em through the mud and locked 'em up. The people said the pump was gonna hurt the river. I guess they were right."

The fishermen's voices faded away as the current took them downstream toward the spawning beds.

Zak looked at his watch. "Come on, Ziggy. Let's get going.

Ivy'll find us. She knows where we fish."

For over a hundred years the weeping willow had swept out over the water's edge. Its thick old roots, nurtured by the river, grew close to the surface of the rich, black soil. This was Zak's favorite place in the whole world. After setting his knapsack down under the tree, he reached in and pulled out a plastic container of worms. He baited his line, cast out into the river and, with high hopes, sat down to wait for a fish to bite.

Ziggy dug a hole nearby and curled up in it to take a nap.

With wonder in his big, dark eyes, Zak watched the sunlight shimmering on the rapids. The sun's rays felt warm on his face. A fish swam by and tiny little bubbles rose and sparkled on the surface of the water. Across the way, high in the palisades above the riverbank, the icicles that had formed through winter were melting. The water glistened as it trickled down the ancient rocks. Zak could hear the breeze wrestling with the trees, and the branches crackling. He leaned back and nestled his head into the massive old trunk.

Suddenly a huge gust of wind swept up the river and, with a loud "CRACK," a branch broke free and came crashing down from the willow.

THE MAGIC BUBBLE

"**Z**ak! Zak! Wake up! Are you all right?" Zak opened his eyes. Ivy was shaking his shoulder and Ziggy was licking his forehead.

His forehead! He quickly brought his hand up to his face and felt a big bump just above his left eye. "Ow!" he yelled.

Lying next to him, over his knapsack, was a branch from the old willow. It had knocked his fishing rod out of his hands and covered him with twigs.

"Wow," he said, holding his head, "that was a close one!"

"Yeah," said Ivy, "you were lucky. Are you all right?"

Zak pulled himself up. "Ah, it's just a bump on the head," he said, and looked at his watch. "But where were you? You're always late!"

"I couldn't help it. My grandma came over this morning—and look what she brought!" Ivy held up a big bottle of bubbles.

"But where's your fishing rod?" he asked. "I thought we were gonna fish today!"

"Oh, Zak," she sighed, "we can fish any day. Let's blow bubbles! Look, there's a pipe and a wand—and they're magic! It says it right here on the bottle."

"That's just soap and water, Ivy. They're not magic," Zak said, annoyed. "Stop dreaming!"

"Don't tell me I can't dream, Zachary," she answered. "Anyway, you can still keep your line in the river. You can do both."

"Oh, all right," Zak answered. He always gave in to his friend.

"Here—you take the pipe and I'll take the wand," she said.

She unscrewed the cap, and they took turns dipping into the bottle and blowing bubbles. Ziggy was jumping around, trying to pop them.

"Look how beautiful they are," said Ivy. "They're like big round rainbows."

The bubbles drifted out over the river and floated up into the trees.

Zak stopped for a moment and just watched, his eyes following the bubbles high into the blue sky until they finally broke and, with a soundless pop, disappeared.

A cloud passed over the sun and the sky grew very dark. The wind picked up, the branches on the trees roared and the birds sang louder than ever before. Then, out of nowhere, a sparkling giant of a bubble appeared! It was unlike any Zak had ever seen, and it started to circle downward, turning in the breeze. As it came closer and closer, it got bigger and bigger and then, to the children's complete amazement, it started to spin! First it spun ten times to the right and then it spun ten times to the left.

"Zak, what's happening?" cried Ivy.

Ziggy growled and hunched down next to Zak. They all stared at the bubble as it grew brighter and brighter against the blackening sky. Colors raced across its surface like lightning and, with one great earthshaking flash, the bubble hit the ground and disappeared.

A strange and delightful-looking creature stood right in front of the awestruck children!

The creature was clearly not of this world, though he had an almost human air about him. He was slender and a little bit taller than the children. His immense, egg-shaped head was tipped with a thin, grass-green beard on his chin, and bushy green eyebrows over huge, almond-shaped, aquamarine eyes—the color of the sea! But the oddest things about him were his long ears. They were bright green—all four of them! The two outer ears hung down on the side of his head and the other two grew up from the top alongside a green-stemmed antenna with a golden yellow tip, like a flower. Clenched in his pearly white teeth was a long pipe with three large bird feathers hanging from the bowl. Along the stem of the pipe was a row of ten little buttons, each one a different color, and they were all blinking on and off.

The agitated visitor was wiping a grimy mess off his clothes. His white polka dot tunic and open-toed, fish-scaled boots were wet and dirty and streaked with greasy black oil.

The shocked children and little dog remained frozen where they stood. Their mouths fell open when the bizarre character grumbled under his breath.

Zak's eyes were drawn to the shiny buckle on the creature's belt. It seemed to be some sort of medallion, a golden ball surrounded by interlocking circles of silver and copper. The belt was like a rainbow-colored carpenter's belt, with red, blue, purple, yellow and orange loops. In one of the loops was a crystal-clear glass bottle, and in another was a tattered, rolled-up old magazine.

The being stopped trying to clean himself off and with a frustrated grunt, straightened up and pulled the pipe from his mouth. He tapped the bowl on the palm of his hand. A few drops of water fell out and before they even touched the ground, they lit up like sparklers on the Fourth of July.

Zak and Ivy watched, dumbfounded, as he reached down to his side with the pipe. As it came closer to the belt the little buttons began brilliantly flashing and when he placed it into the purple loop, his buckle sent off an enormous clap of thunder and a blinding burst of light.

Terrified, Zak grabbed Ivy's hand and they dove behind the trunk of the old willow. Ziggy let out a shrill yelp and leaped up to attack the bolt of light. But the great ray vanished into thin air as quickly as it had come, leaving the animal directly facing the strange visitor!

Without hesitation, the creature looked down and firmly asked the dog, "Are you the one in charge here?"

Ziggy looked up from sniffing the stranger's feet and cocked his head. He wagged his tail and raised his paw.

The creature bent down and, with all the gentleness in the world, held the little dog's face between his hands. "Oh," he said, "I see." As the creature spoke, his palms gave off a pale, warm glow and his large, intense, aquamarine eyes slowly changed color to a soft lavender blue. "You're the earthling of loyalty—the humans' best friend."

Ziggy kissed him on the nose.

The children were peeking out from behind the willow.

"Did you see that, Zak?" Ivy asked. "His eyes changed color and his hands glowed! How did he do that? Is he a magician? Is that real magic?"

"I don't know, Ivy. Maybe he's an extraterrestrial."

Ivy shuddered. "Do you really think so?"

The mystical stranger abruptly stood and folded his arms behind him. He began pacing back and forth.

"Well then," he demanded of Ziggy, his eyes flaring to a bright green, "where are the Guardian Residents of this planet? Are they the humans? Where did they run to and who is in charge here?"

Shaking in his sneakers, Zak gathered his composure and courageously stepped forward from behind the tree. In a quivering voice he said, "I am."

Quietly his dark-skinned, curly-haired friend inched her way up to his side.

Zak gulped. "I mean, we are," he corrected himself.

Ivy's green eyes were as wide as saucers, but she stood up straight and, stepping forward, she demanded, "Who are you? What are you? I'm Ivy, and this is Zak, and . . . and . . . what can we do for you?"

Before the creature could answer, Zak interjected, "Yeah, are you a UFO or something?"

"A what?"

"You know, an unidentified flying object."

"What? What do you mean? I'm identifiable! I'm undeniable! I'm Professor Aquius Botanicus Angelicus and I've come to your planet for clean water!"

ANGELICUS OF QUANTIA

"**W**ater?" Zak looked puzzled. "Are you thirsty? My mom packed me some juice in my thermos, if you want it."

Angelicus smiled. "No, no, no!" he exclaimed. "That's awfully sharing of you, but I need water for my pipe."

"Well, there's lots of water right here in the river, Professor ...uh ..." Zak scratched his head. "Ang ... Ang ... what did you say your name was? And where did you say you're from?"

Angelicus' ears flattened down around his head. "I didn't say where I was from," he said firmly, "but never mind that. Do you children call that river clean?"

"Well, it's cleaner than it was. They've been cleaning it up. The fish are back," Zak responded.

"Oh, rubbish!" Angelicus' eyes slowly scanned the surface of the water. "What's that?" He pointed at a plastic soda bottle bobbing just offshore. "The river can't eat it, can't drink it! Can't send it up and make a cloud out of it!"

Ivy ran down the bank. Ziggy followed her. She picked up a branch that had fallen from a nearby sycamore tree and, reaching out with it, maneuvered the bottle toward the water's edge. Trying to help, Ziggy grabbed onto the branch too. Finally she brought the bottle close enough to pull it out and took it up to a trashcan near the canoe rental office.

Angelicus looked at Zak with a melancholy expression on his face. He shook his head from side to side and twitched his nose. "I must be on the wrong planet," he said.

"What planet are you looking for, Professor?" asked Zak.

"The Big Blue Ball. Its occupants call it the planet Earth. I was sure my bubble was on course. I followed the stars to your galaxy. I found your sun, looked to your clouds and listened to your wind. And this place certainly looks like a Big Blue Ball to me."

"Well, this is the planet Earth, Professor Ang ...?" Zak said, struggling for the name again.

"Angelicus. Aquius Botanicus Angelicus of Quantia. Well, if this is the planet Earth, there must be something terribly, terribly wrong! Because this river is not as clean as it should be." He reached down to the red loop on his belt and pulled out the old magazine.

He mumbled to himself as he thumbed through the pages. "Now, where was that? Ah, here! It's right here in the *Planetary Guide*." He read: 'The Big Blue Ball is not too hot, not too cold. It has sun, rain, wind and snow, is abundant with living creatures and has the largest supply of water in the universe. Its lakes, ponds, streams, rivers and oceans are all clean and contain plenty of pure water for charging a traveler's pipe.' You see? The perfect water to spark my bubble with. It has the power to guide me back home to Quantia."

Ivy and Ziggy had returned. Ivy, fascinated by the professor's words, asked, "What's Quantia, Professor Angelicus?"

"Why, Quantia is the Rainbow Planet. You could say it's in the center of the universe, in the flash between moments of time and space. It was created out of water and light, at the very place where the light meets and shimmers off the water. Some of us call it the Land of Sparkle. You can look into the windows of Quantia from here. You can see it from almost anywhere, if you look hard enough."

"We can?" cried the children. "How?"

In a gentle voice, he said as he pointed: "Look at the sun sparkling on the river. Look at the dewdrops glistening on the trees. Walk through a puddle of rain, and when the sun comes out, you'll see it. You can even see it in the eyes of your fellow earthlings when they laugh!" And with that, he let out the deepest, heartiest laugh the children had ever heard, and his eyes twinkled like a thousand blue stars on a clear winter night.

He walked down to the river and looked out, absorbing the beauty. "Extraordinary!" he exclaimed. "Extra, extraordinary! This is a wonderful river. So deep—so wide—a home to so many creatures."

At that, a fish jumped high, its scales shimmering a silvery blue in the morning light.

"Hello, little fellow," Angelicus called gently. He cocked his head to the sound of the current, murmuring over the rocks, as if the river was talking to him. Then he bent down and scooped up some water in his hands, and the sparkle left his eyes.

"But I'm sorry to say, something has happened to this water. Unnatural intruders have invaded it, and it's lost some of its power. Nitrogen! Pesticides! And there's not quite enough oxygen. But thank the stars it still can sparkle. Thank goodness, it's still alive. Not like the hopeless planet, Nega."

"Nega," Ivy gasped. "I've never heard of Nega."

The professor's eyes changed to a cloudy gray. "Nega is no more," he sadly proclaimed. "The only way you'll learn about Nega will be in the Universal History books. I've just come from there. That's where my clothes got so dirty. I was sent there by the Grand Council to help save the planet, but I was too late."

"What do you mean, Professor?" asked Zak.

"Nega was once one of the most beautiful planets in the universe. Why, it had almost as much water as your planet has. But over the centuries the Guardian Residents got more and more caught up in their own crazy inventions. They didn't think of anything else. Their minds created all kinds of fancy machines and complicated gadgets. I don't even know how they did it. Simply mind boggling!"

With a deep frown, Angelicus sadly shook his head. "But with all that, they completely forgot the most important natural creation of all. They totally ignored and abused it." He paused. "Can you imagine not taking care of the water? Thinking they could live without it."

The children looked at each other. "If there wasn't any water, we'd sure be thirsty," said Zak.

Ziggy's mouth fell open and he started to pant.

Ivy said, "Yeah. That would be terrible! We couldn't take

showers or go swimming. The dishwasher wouldn't even work."

Suddenly Zak saw the whole picture. "There wouldn't be anyplace for the ducks or the fish to live. And what about the whales and the octopuses? All the things that live in the ocean!"

"Without water, the flowers and trees couldn't grow. There wouldn't be any rain. There wouldn't be any snow," Ivy went on.

"You can't live without it," Angelicus agreed solemnly. "It was the most precious resource their planet had, but they took it for granted."

"Well, what happened? What happened to them?" Ivy asked.

"They used the water—just selfishly used the water. Never thought about its needs and desires. Slowly it became sick and polluted. The water could only take so much and finally," he paused, "finally it just turned black and died."

"Did . . . did everybody die?" asked Zak.

"No, not everyone. I managed to transport the last remaining few to a neighboring planet in my bubble."

Ivy's eyes filled up with tears. Ziggy whimpered.

Zak asked, heavy hearted, "How many did you save, Professor?"

The professor's eyes looked down to the ground. "Oh. Not enough, not nearly enough. Maybe a million or two creatures."

Zak looked puzzled. "You can do all that in a bubble?"

"Well, Zak, a bubble can do most anything. The purer the water, the more a bubble can do—the farther a bubble can go. But only the purest of pure water can take me home to Quantia."

Pointing to the empty bottle on his belt, he said, "You see, I can only carry a limited supply. I used so much at Nega. I only had enough to get here to your planet. But if the *Planetary Guide* says your Big Blue Ball has crystal-clear water to spark my bubble with, it must be here somewhere. Your river certainly has enough power to take us around the Big Blue Ball . . . even your galaxy. Where do you think we can find the purest water on the planet? Do you think you can help?"

"Does that mean we get to ride in the bubble?" asked Zak.

"Well, sure," said Angelicus.

Ivy yelled, "No way!"

"Way!" smiled Angelicus. "How else would we get around?"

Ziggy barked. He couldn't wait to go inside a bubble!

"Thanks, kids. I wouldn't want to miss the Rainbow Festival," said the professor.

"The Rainbow Festival? What's that?" yelled the kids.

The professor's eyes turned a deep purple. "Ah, that's when all the Sharelings—that's how we call ourselves—come together to celebrate the beauty of our planet and give thanks to the Great Universal Source for creating us. Not that we don't take a moment every day to give thanks, but on that particular day we all join together to celebrate the delicate balance of nature . . . the gift of life to all living things, big and small. We realized a long time ago that one c\an't live without the other.

"Giant rainbows fill our skies," he continued, "our waters sparkle as brightly as a billion diamonds and reflect back all the way to our suns. And our whole solar system lights up in sixteen point seven million colors! It only happens once every billion years. Quantian time, of course. So you see why I have to get home."

Ivy sighed and said, "Quantia sounds like a beautiful place."

Zak got a dreamy look in his eyes. "Boy! I'd like to see it. I'd like to go there."

"Well, Zak, maybe you can someday," Angelicus said gently.

"I'd like to meet the Sharelings." The boy thought for a minute. "Why are you called Sharelings, anyway? Does that mean you share stuff? Like, do you share your games and your lunch?"

"Yes. We share our food and water, our feelings and our love. We share everything. We share the space on our planet equally. We're all friends on Quantia and we all speak the same language. The animals talk, the trees, the flowers . . . even the rivers sing." He smiled. "In harmony, of course. You become a Shareling by doing what you can do best."

Ziggy wagged his tail. He knew what the professor was talking about.

Suddenly Angelicus said, "Enough of this, we've got work to do!"

"What should we do, Professor?" asked Zak.

"Why, go, of course!" he answered, and looked at the kids. "Where would you look for pure water?"

Zak shouted, "I know! We can go down to the bay. If we follow the river, it'll take us to the bay. My grandparents have a summer house there. I'll show you."

"That's salt water, Zak," said Ivy. "He means fresh water."

Angelicus interrupted. "Salt water is good. I'd like to see this salt water. I'd like to go there."

Ziggy approved. He barked and wagged his tail. He loved the bay.

"Well then, I'd better get to work," Angelicus said. "We're not going anywhere without a bubble." He waded into the river.

The morning mist had long since disappeared; it had been absorbed into the atmosphere. The sky was deep blue, the air crystal clear, and the sunlight sparkled brilliantly on the water.

CHAPTER THREE

Angelicus took a deep breath. He enjoyed smelling the birth of spring. He stood there in the middle of the river, his big aquamarine eyes gleaming like bright gemstones against the backdrop of the palisades.

Angelicus bent down and dipped his pipe into the sparkle.

BUBBLE POWER

Professor Angelicus walked up the riverbank, pipe in hand. "All right, Ivy, Zak. The pipe's ready. Let's get the bubble going!" he exclaimed.

"What do we do, Professor?" Zak asked. He was a little nervous, but didn't want to show it.

Ivy whispered to Zak, "I'm a little scared."

Zak took his friend by the hand and said, "Don't worry, Ivy. This is gonna be awesome!"

Angelicus overheard them. He said, "Just stand on either side of me and don't worry about a thing. The wind knows exactly what we're doing. All the life forces of nature are here with us."

The children moved in close to him.

"But what makes the bubble go?" asked Ivy. "How does it stay up?"

"Well, think of it this way," he said. "The sun is our engine, the wind our navigator, and the water is our fuel. That's the secret of Bubble Power." He paused. "Now, I'll answer all your other questions once I get us off the ground."

Focusing intently on his pipe, the professor fiddled with the buttons. As the lights blinked on and off, he took a deep, deep breath, put the instrument to his mouth and blew. A giant bubble slowly expanded from out of the pipe's bowl and a great, swirling sheet of iridescent light completely surrounded the adventurous trio.

"Ziggy! Where's Ziggy?" Zak yelled.

From behind the transparent rainbow film of the bubble, the children could hear him barking ferociously at something hidden in the brush.

"Ziggy! Ziggy, come on. You're gonna miss the bubble," the children called out with all their might.

The dog growled and bared his teeth, then turned and raced back toward the bubble.

"Come on, Ziggy. What's wrong with you?" Zak shouted and put out his hands.

With a howl, Ziggy jumped right through the bubble's skin and landed, panting, in Zak's arms. The hole closed up immediately behind him.

To their surprise, the children felt an invisible floor form beneath their feet. Then, without warning, the bubble lifted a few inches off the ground.

"OK," said Angelicus, "this is the tricky part."

Gingerly, Angelicus removed the pipe from his mouth. It

still remained attached to the inside of the bubble's surface and, as he released his grip, the pipe instantly sprang forward to the front of the compartment. Lodged there in an upright position it looked just like the gearshift on an old car.

A mechanical voice called out, "Prepare for takeoff. Prepare for takeoff."

Startled, Ivy asked, "Who's that?"

"Oh, that's just the voice of the pipe," said Angelicus, "keeping us informed and updated."

Grasping the pipe and carefully pulling back on it, Angelicus yelled, "Here we go. Keep your feet firmly on the floor."

Within a few seconds, the wind blew in from the east and the bubble started to spin. It spun ten times to the left, then the wind shifted and blew from the west and it spun ten times to the right. Slowly they rose into the air.

Zak stepped toward Ivy and his body became weightless like an astronaut. He floated around the cabin with Ziggy squirming in his arms!

"I told you to stay steady," scolded Angelicus. He pushed a button on the pipe and it seemed to Zak as if the floor reached up and grabbed him by the feet.

In an instant Zak was standing upright at Ivy's side.

"I can't believe this is happening!" he exclaimed.

Ivy looked at him. "I told you bubbles were magic, Zak."

Angelicus grinned.

Ziggy jumped free from Zak's arms and floated over to the edge of the bubble to peer down at the river. The children watched through the invisible floor as the bubble climbed smoothly into the air. The craft rose to the top of the stately old ash tree and, as it passed, Zak saw a cross-eyed crow staring at the strange sight. It ruffled its purplish black feathers and called out—four loud caws. For a split second, Zak felt it was looking straight at him.

"Zak, I can see the mill," yelled Ivy. "And there's the old barn. . . . Look how much bigger it is than the other houses."

"Look at the creek, Ivy, look! It changes color where it meets the river. And look over there—that's my house!" Zak pointed excitedly.

After they had risen a little farther, the bubble came to an abrupt halt and hung, suspended in midair. With a yelp, Ziggy fell to the floor.

Alarmed, Zak asked, "What's wrong? Is there a problem, Professor?"

Angelicus smiled. "No, no, no," he said, "I'm aligning the bubble."

Ivy looked at him. "Align? What does that mean?"

"If the bubble isn't centered and our energy isn't flowing in the same direction as the rest of the universe, the bubble can't generate enough power to move more than a few feet. So I have to align us all together," he explained. "Then we can go with the natural flow."

The children looked confused.

"Well, don't think about it. You'll understand soon enough. Just stand still and I'll show you. First, close your eyes."

The professor turned to Zak (now standing straight with eyes closed) and placed his hands on Zak's temples. Ivy couldn't help but peek. The professor's eyes were shining like two clear crystal balls and his hands began to glow. A white light appeared over his head and flowed down in waves around his body until he was completely enveloped in a mystical glow. Ivy watched the bump on Zak's forehead disappear.

Zak felt the strangest sensation . . . as if a warm sun had begun to rise down deep inside of him. He felt tall and strong like the giant ash, as solid and secure as a huge boulder. He felt free and light as a deer gliding and bounding through open, golden fields with Ziggy at his side. He felt peaceful . . . happy.

With a start, he opened his eyes, realizing he had returned to normal, only somehow different. "What was that, Professor? What was I feeling?"

Angelicus smiled. "You were just feeling your own powers. You were feeling the center of your existence. Now your body, mind and spirit are balanced. You've been aligned. Doesn't it feel wonderful?"

"Yeah," said Zak, with a dreamy look on his face.

The professor turned to Ivy and, as his hands neared her face, she felt the delicate beat of her own heart. Her eyes were closed but it seemed like she could see forever. She could touch the clouds with her fingertips. She heard a chorus of stars singing in harmony. As one shooting star crossed her line of vision, she rode on it into the galaxies. Her hair was blowing in a soft galactic breeze and she felt the spray of silver dust on her face.

"Could this be my soul I'm feeling?" she wondered. "Am I visiting heaven?"

As she opened her eyes, Angelicus smiled and said, "In a way, you are, Ivy."

And she sort of understood.

The two young friends looked at each other in awe, and their big brown eyes locked together for a moment. Ziggy barked and broke their trance.

"What about Ziggy? Doesn't he need to be aligned?" asked Zak.

"No, no." The professor laughed. "Ziggy's always aligned. Just like all the other creatures on your planet. Now," he continued, "don't let yourselves get flustered. Everything's going to seem a little different to you. We're in Bubble Time now."

"Bubble Time?" The children grew more amazed with each minute.

"Bubble Time. Up till now, your clocks ticked to the rhythm of your planet revolving around your sun. But now you've been aligned to the heartbeat of the universe. The clock in the bubble ticks in time to the twinkle of the stars. In the universe there really isn't any time at all, so we can go as slowly as we want or as quickly as we please. We can go faster or slower than Earth time.

"We can travel in and out of the seasons, if we want. Summer? Why, just think about it. Winter? Feel the frost bite your nose. Fall? You're a leaf of red and gold, swirling and floating through the autumn air. It's all up to you. It depends on how you feel inside. Imagine there are no boundaries, no limits. You can go wherever your imagination will take you."

The professor turned to his pipe. "Now just sit down and make yourselves comfortable," he said over his shoulder.

Ivy asked, "Where do we sit, Professor?"

"Anywhere you'd like. Just trust yourself and the seat will be there for you."

The next thing Ivy knew, she was seated in a pale pink rocking chair. Painted all over it were little red apples, and the cushion was made of delicate white lace. "How did you do that?" she demanded.

"I didn't do it, you did," laughed the professor. "Have you ever seen that chair before?"

Ivy looked down at the chair. "Why, yes," she said, "I saw this in a store window and I've wanted it ever since!"

"You see?" he said. "Just trust yourself."

Zak found himself sinking comfortably into his father's favorite stuffed chair. Ziggy dug into an old rag rug, curled up, and went to sleep.

"Everyone ready?" asked Angelicus. He pulled back on the pipe.

"Ready, Professor," the children's voices rang with enthusiasm.

The wind blew from the north, and the bubble circled around to the left and headed down the river.

A SUMMER STORM

The shimmering, transparent craft drifted southward with its unlikely passengers, following the meandering course of the river. The children watched as the professor's explanation of time suddenly came to life.

Miraculously, the season began to change before their eyes, brilliantly painting the valley below. Yellow forsythia and daffodils budded and bloomed, giving way to patches of multicolored tulips and lavender specks of phlox and hyacinth. The treetops were covered with chartreuse buds that instantly matured and burst into numerous shades of green. White and pink cherry blossoms of spring were tenderly falling like soft snowflakes over flowers of summer that were popping up from beneath the earth.

"Look, Professor, my watch is going haywire!" Zak exclaimed. The hands were spinning around the dial faster and faster, until they were nothing but a blur. "I guess it's still on Earth time."

Angelicus nodded. "Some things can never go into Bubble Time. Every living thing has the power to flow back and forth through time at will. But a gadget like that is only designed to help humans organize their time. So it's bound to Earth forever."

Ivy, oblivious to their conversation, exclaimed, "This is beyond belief! Zak, do you see what's going on down there?"

"Yeah," he mumbled. But he was still staring at the hands spinning around the dial.

"Zak, look," she insisted.

Zak pulled his eyes away from the watch and looked down through the bubble.

"This *is* extremely excellent," he agreed.

Angelicus smiled broadly. "Yes indeed. You folks certainly have one of the most beautiful planets I've ever seen," he said.

Ziggy woke up and wagged his tail. He loved his home, the Earth.

As the bubble rose higher and higher, two turkey buzzards soared above them in the warm blue sky. Their small red heads nodded as they gracefully glided and rocked on the air currents rising up from the valley floor. One of them spotted the craft and dove down to take a better look. Pulling up to a near stop next to the startled occupants, he spread out his giant wings, almost engulfing the craft. He stared in and suddenly began to speak!

"Yo," he croaked, "Professor Angelicus. We heard you were around." He flapped his wings again to steady himself and cocked his gawky head. "What brings you to Earth?"

"Well, my boy," called out Angelicus, "I've come to refuel my pipe. My young friends here have offered to help me find the pure water I need, and we're headed down to the bay to look. Listen, you fellows are part of the sanitation department, aren't you? How is the water down there?" he asked.

"Well, it could be better, Professor," said the buzzard.

"I was sort of afraid you'd say that." Angelicus looked disappointed.

"But hey, check it out. You might get lucky," the bird quickly offered. "If you don't, let us know. We'll be around."

"Thanks, I'll keep that in mind," said Angelicus with a big, warm smile.

"You do that," croaked the buzzard. "Now I gotta get back to work." With a flap of his giant wings, he lofted high into the air to rejoin his friend.

"Did you hear that, Zak?" Ivy whispered. "That turkey buzzard talked!"

"Yeah," Zak responded under his breath, "I thought only parrots could talk."

Angelicus' ears stood up straight and he spun around. "Talked? Sure he talked. All Sharelings talk. You've just started to listen a little better, that's all." He twitched his nose and returned to his controls.

The bubble floated down the valley. A patchwork quilt of gold and green fields spread out beneath them. Herds of grazing deer dotted the landscape. As the adventurers turned a bend in the river and passed over a cluster of trees, a spectacular field of sunflowers appeared below, their majestic heads all facing up toward the sun.

"Wow!" said Zak. "I've never seen that before. Can we slow down, Professor?"

Angelicus pulled back on the pipe, the bubble slowed to a crawl and they descended toward the sea of sunny yellow faces. Suddenly, as if on some unheard command, the flowers closed their petals and, in perfect formation, drooped their brilliant heads. In a matter of seconds all were facing the ground and the field turned from yellow to green.

Alarmed, Ivy cried out, "What's happening? Why did they do that? Did we disturb them?"

Ziggy began to shake and he jumped up to bury his head in Zak's lap.

"Professor, Ziggy only does this when it thunders," said Zak.

"Well, it must be time to feed the Sharelings of your planet," said the professor.

"What do you mean?"

"Water. It's time for watering. Your Big Blue Ball has great and wondrous powers. Every living thing is interconnected. Before the water comes, the air changes, and everyone senses it in one way or another. You see? The flowers closed their petals and Ziggy tried to find cover. They knew."

"Do you mean it's gonna rain? And they knew? Without the weatherman?" asked Ivy.

"I remember when my great-grandfather used to say he could feel it in his bones," said Zak. " 'It's gonna rain today,' he used to say."

"Of course he did," Angelicus said.

Abruptly the sun disappeared behind an immense black cloud. A monstrous bolt of lightning streaked across the sky and the bubble shook with an enormous clap of thunder. The wind wailed from the west and a torrential rain pounded down on the bubble. Within seconds the little sphere was being buffeted wildly by the intensity of the summer storm. The occupants held on for dear life.

"Is the bubble in trouble, Professor?" Zak asked, frightened. "Are we gonna crash?"

"It takes an awful lot to hurt a bubble," Angelicus affirmed.

But just as he said that, they all heard a sizzling on the roof of the craft, and a drop of liquid seeped through the top and landed, sputtering on the invisible floor of the cabin.

Suddenly the pipe seemed to go crazy! Colored lights were blinking on and off, racing up and down the stem. Sirens and whistles and blaring music like a carousel gone out of control filled the children's ears. The pipe's voice kept repeating, "Out of balance, out of balance."

Dumbfounded, the children looked to the professor for an explanation. But, to their amazement, he began laughing hysterically. His eyes changed to a muddy brown and his upper ears slammed shut around the flower on his head. Doubling over, he clutched his belly and lost his grip on the floor. In an instant he was floating willy-nilly around the cabin.

Horrified, Ivy shouted, "Professor! Professor! How can you laugh at a time like this?"

"Oh! Hah, hah, hah . . . Oh! Oh! Quick! Take the controls!" wheezed Angelicus. "The rain . . . ah, the rain . . . too much acid in the rain . . . must be . . . nitrous oxide in the rain . . . laughing gas . . . Quantians can't take it . . . the controls . . . pull back . . . we must get above the clouds!"

Zak lunged for the pipe, Ziggy fell from his lap, Ivy lost her balance, and they all joined the professor flailing around in the air. Zak could feel the blood rushing to his face as he grabbed the controls. He pulled back with all his might, but the bubble took a nosedive and began tumbling downward toward the field of flowers, spinning around and around and turning upside down. Then, out of nowhere, a howling gust of wind raged up from below. With a roar, the clouds parted above them and in a whirlwind they were spirited up, up through the storm. Through the thunderhead they raced; then through another layer of billowing white clouds and higher still, till finally, with one big BOOM, the bubble rocketed past the last thin layers of the Earth's atmosphere and out into space.

"Whoa," yelled Angelicus, "we don't have to go to the moon! We just had to get out of that rain." He was back to his old self, standing upright and chuckling at the sight of Zak's serious expression as the boy clutched the pipe to his chest. Angelicus reached over. "You can relax now, Zak," he said. He took back the controls and brought the craft to a halt. "Good job. I couldn't have done it better myself."

"Professor, are you all right?" Ivy asked. She floated down to her rocking chair and pulled Ziggy into her lap.

"Yes, I'm fine now, thank you, Ivy," said Angelicus.

"What happened?" asked Zak.

"Well, I guess I just wasn't thinking. I've heard about that phenomenon. You must still burn fossil fuels, like coal and oil, on your planet. When they burn they release chemicals that bond with the water in the air, and turn the rain into a kind of acid—quite toxic to us Quantians. We don't handle it very well. I should have been prepared and changed the settings on the pipe."

He looked closely at the children, his eyes lavender blue.

"But I feel quite chipper now, don't worry." He turned to the pipe and pushed a few buttons.

The pipe played a little melody and said, "Balance restored."

The lights dimmed and the children stared out into space.

BEYOND THE BIG BLUE BALL

"Look, Ivy, we're just like astronauts! We're in the Milky Way! I bet that's Venus over there. And look at Mars—it's red, just like in my books." Excitedly, Zak pointed at the Earth. "It really is a Big Blue Ball, Professor. Just like you said . . . blue and green. But it's so much smaller than I ever imagined."

Ivy sighed. "Ooh, it is. Like a sparkling blue jewel on a black velvet cushion." She held up Ziggy. "See, Ziggy?"

The little dog wagged his tail, his black eyes shining, and licked her on the face.

"Jewel is right, Ivy," intoned the professor. "A living planet is a precious thing."

"It's nothing like my globe at home," remarked Zak. "I can't see the borders of the countries. And they aren't different colors or anything."

"Borders? Borders?" The professor looked bewildered. He thought for a minute, then pulled the *Planetary Guide* from his belt. He turned rapidly through the pages and then stopped and said, "Aha, here we are. 'Borders: imaginary lines (sometimes following the natural shape of a planet) established by some early warlike Guardian Residents to separate individual groups of their species from each other. An ancient practice thought to be extinct throughout the universe.' Isn't that interesting . . . hard to imagine."

He scratched his lower right ear and a puzzled look came over his face. "If they separate themselves from each other and divide up the planet, how can they feel whole? How can they share ideas?" He turned to the children. "I'll definitely have to put this in my log. You're sure you have borders?"

The children nodded.

"Absolutely fascinating! The other Sharelings of your planet . . . do they use these borders?"

"What do you mean?" asked Zak.

"Do the birds? Can the plant creatures see them? The water doesn't stop at these borders, does it?"

The children shook their heads.

"Well, this is certainly one for the books. The Grand Council of Quantia will be amazed. In fact, they'll be astounded!"

Suddenly a huge, radiant beam of light, as brilliant as a hundred million stars, flared out from the great depths of the black sea of space.

"Professor, what's that?" the children yelled.

Ziggy howled.

The professor turned around to look. "Oh, that's just the light from a supernova," he said, matter of factly. "The breath of a star. I'm sure you can see them from Earth. They don't happen that often, but when they do, they shine so bright you can see them for many days and nights."

Ivy sighed. "Like the Star of Bethlehem at Christmas."

Angelicus tapped himself on the forehead. "Let me see now. I recognize those colors. I remember that star. It exploded right here in your galaxy. About eleven thousand years ago, Earth time."

Ivy's mouth fell open. "Eleven thousand years ago?" She could hardly believe it.

"Well, light doesn't move as fast as you might think. You're just seeing it now. I bet a whole lot of new little worlds sprouted up from that stardust by now."

"What do you mean, 'new worlds,' Professor?" Zak asked, staring intently at the light.

"Why, just that. If a star didn't breathe once in a while, all the worlds we know wouldn't get a chance to form. The ant world, the plant world, the water world, the world of light. From the smallest rock out here in space to all the planets in the universe."

Ivy interrupted. "A star breathes?"

"The whole universe breathes. And when it does, all the heavenly bodies sputter, sparkle, burst, quake and flash. A supernova is a kind of sputter—a small version of the first Big Breath of the universe. The Great Universal Source took a giant deep breath and when it exhaled, it blew life and light into all living things. Everything and everyone is made of starlight and stardust. Your Earth itself was once a hot star seed. And in it was everything a planet needs to grow. So even you come from the stars."

"Stars? We're made of stars? Is Ziggy?" Ivy was star struck.

"Are you made of stars, Professor Angelicus?" asked Zak. "Is Quantia?"

"Absolutely. Nothing more and nothing less," the professor affirmed. "The iron in your blood, the calcium in your bones. Everything, even the tiniest drop of water shining on a spider's web is stardust and starlight. All living things are related. We're all brothers and sisters."

He pointed out toward the silent brilliance in space, his large eyes clear and luminescent. "We were all created in the intergalactic clouds that came from the first great breath of life. Some call it the Essence of God."

Ziggy wagged his tail and his eyes sparkled. He understood what the professor was saying.

The children gazed intensely at the spectacular blazing star, the professor's words fading away from their ears. Hypnotized by the light, Ivy felt tranquil. She reached out for Zak. He took her hand and, side-by-side, the two friends felt their spirits lift away toward the light, leaving the bubble behind them.

Like feathers, they glided on a serene galactic breeze, spinning and whirling through enormous, bright, glowing clouds. They moved faster and faster, beyond the speed of light, shooting through boundless clusters of stars on their magical journey toward the center of the galaxy. Their senses opened wide, absorbing the great magnitude of the cosmos.

"Zak," Ivy thought out loud, "this is wonderful, but what's happening?"

"I don't know, but it sure feels astronomical," Zak's thoughts echoed through space.

They heard a giant chuckle. In an instant, they were spiraling back toward the bubble. They could see Angelicus and Ziggy and two children below them.

"Look Ivy," yelled Zak, "that's *us* down there!"

In a blink of an eye, the children were back in their bodies.

"What . . . what happened?" Zak forced the words out of his panting lungs.

"Yeah, Professor, where were we? How did we do that?" blurted out Ivy.

Angelicus' eyes were aquamarine again and the flower on his antenna glowed. "You seem to have discovered a starpath," he said quietly.

"Starpath?" Ivy repeated.

"Um-humh. You took a short excursion on one of your starpaths—your inner roads. You have many of them inside you . . . as many as there are stars. They're the sacred pathways that lead you through life and they're paved with spirit and love. When you follow the spark in your heart and believe in yourself, you can go anywhere, do anything. You were concentrating so deeply, your spirit focused and you followed a starlit path to the supernova. Be patient. You'll learn more about it as time goes on."

Abruptly he turned, pushed a few buttons and pulled back on the controls. "Now it's time to get going," he said. "We're not going to find any water out here."

"But, Professor . . ." Ivy protested.

"In time," he said, "everything in its right time."

It was clear he would say nothing more on the subject. Ivy and Zak looked at each other and shrugged.

The bubble took a dip and the pipe called out, "Gravitational field ahead. Gravitational field. Take your positions."

The children returned to their chairs. Ziggy lay down on his old rag rug and made himself comfortable.

As the bubble traveled toward Earth, Zak and Ivy noticed a large metal object with rectangular, silver wings. The object was silently looming in space as they moved closer. Small metallic squares covered its surface.

"Look, Ivy. There's a weather satellite," said Zak. "We just learned about that in school."

Angelicus looked around quizzically at them.

"You know, Professor," said Ivy, "for watching the weather patterns. So we can forecast tornados and hurricanes and stuff."

"Ah," replied Angelicus, "a very hopeful sign for your Guardian Residents. Primitive technology, to be sure, but it's good that you've come outside to look at your planet. Once you see the whole picture, it's easier to understand how much everything is a part of everything else. Of course, you have to do a little looking inside, as well."

The children looked at each other and smiled. He talked funny and sure lectured a lot, but they were growing very fond of this odd character.

As they approached the swirling blue planet, the children began to recognize landmarks.

"Zak, there's that volcano in the South Seas! You can see the smoke."

"Yeah. But what's that smoke over there, Ivy?" asked Zak, but quickly realized. "Oh. That must be the rain forest. Where they're burning the trees."

"Burning the trees?" The words exploded from Angelicus' mouth as his eyes flared to a crimson red. "What do you mean, burning the trees?"

"Well, a lot of people aren't happy about it, Professor," Zak said. "They're trying to stop it."

"I should hope so! When you burn the trees you're burning yourselves! The trees have an important job on a planet like yours. They keep the air sweet with oxygen. They share fruits and nuts and they're home to many Sharelings. They don't mind if you take some of them to build shelter with, but this is going too far. That smoke is awful!"

Quietly, Ivy spoke up. "Our teacher told us that burning the trees puts more acid rain in the atmosphere and creates global warming. So the kids at school plant new trees all the time."

The professor's face brightened up and his eyes softened to a pale green. "Well, that's good, Ivy," he said. "That's very, very hopeful. I'm glad some of your Residents are looking out for the future generations."

The bubble continued downward, floating through the hazy blue line of the Earth's atmosphere. Nighttime was turning into day as they drew close to a city. The lights from the street lamps, billboards and giant buildings were reflecting on the river. They started blinking off one by one as the first pink of sunrise appeared in the east. Zak and Ivy looked up at the fading stars. One shot across the sky.

"Look, Professor, a shooting star!" exclaimed Ivy.

"Ah, you kids better wish on that star. On Quantia we say that any time you see a shooting star, your wish will come true."

"We have that same saying here on Earth," said Zak.

"Well, I can't say I'm surprised!" The professor let out a hearty laugh. His eyes sparkled and all four of his green ears wiggled.

THE CITY

Through the smoggy air, the sun was rising over the city. Cars, trucks and buses were bumper to bumper on the grid-work streets, crisscrossed highways and mammoth bridges that tied the web of the vast metropolis together. An inconceivable din of honking horns echoed in the bubble. Ziggy stood up, walked over and sniffed at the invisible wall of the craft as it drifted down over the river. He growled, then quickly ran back to his rag rug, dug a hole and buried his nose.

Angelicus' nostrils flared and he turned to the little dog. "You're right, Ziggy. That odor is vile—and dangerous! Lead, chlorine, acid, oil! Something is definitely out of balance here."

His eyes scanned the cluttered industrial area below, taking in the abandoned factories, burning dumps and junkyards. The children shrank back as his eyes slowly turned salmon, then bright orange, and finally blazed to a ferocious fire engine red.

"What is going on here?" he exploded.

Ziggy put his paws over his floppy black ears. He knew what was coming. He knew the professor was ready to launch into one of his long tirades and he couldn't bear to hear it. It was just too painful for his sensitive ears. He had heard there were places on the Earth that were messed up. Word had gotten around. His friends had told him. The birds, who traveled back and forth through the seasons, flying everywhere over water and land, had seen it. Bird told Rabbit. Rabbit had been frightened when he told the gentle Deer. And Deer had told Ziggy. Something awful was happening in these places called cities.

The squirrels were gathering more nuts than they needed, afraid there wouldn't be any more trees. Their friends, the frogs, were disappearing and no one knew why. They needed the frogs. They're the ones who sing to the thunder being. Their song brings on the rain.

Everyone was talking about it. They told Ziggy the problem was his friends, the humans. They were taking up more space than the Great Universal Source had allotted them. Turtle said the humans should learn to slow down and look around. Snake said some of their poisons would wake them up soon enough. Spider said not to worry. The humans had created a web and gotten caught in it. But some of them would see their way out. They could see the light, the weaving of the whole universe. And after all, even flying insects knew to go to the light, didn't they?

A perplexed look crossed Zak's face and he turned to his friend. He whispered, "I can hear what Ziggy's thinking."

"So can I!" blurted out Ivy.

Ziggy lifted his head, looked at the children, rolled his sad brown eyes and wagged his tail.

Angelicus nodded his head. "Ziggy's friends certainly know what they're talking about. Something has got to change around here. Look at those broken-down structures. What is their purpose, anyway? If your Guardian Residents can't use them for some good, why don't they tear them down and make room for some of the other Sharelings? Like the ones who lived here before."

Ziggy's thoughts were heard again. "Bears and beavers, wildcats, all kinds of earthlings used to live here. The air was sweet with flowers and vines, and there were deep woods everywhere. The birds remember."

"You see?" said the professor. "I'm sure they'd be happy to move back in. I'm sure the human residents would enjoy it, too, hearing the birds sing and smelling the fresh earth."

They continued south above the massive urban sprawl.

"Great stars! This place goes on forever!" exclaimed Angelicus. "It's ugly and it smells. How can anything live here?"

"Now wait a minute, Professor," Ivy spoke up. "People come from all over the world to live in the city. I visit my grandmother all the time. She takes me to the ballet, and the symphony, and the theatre. The city can be wonderful."

"Oh Ivy, calm down," said Zak, "he's just talking about the factories and pollution. He can't see all the good stuff from up here."

He turned to Angelicus. "There really are some cool things down there, Professor. Great restaurants and museums."

"I apologize, Ivy. Forgive me for being so shortsighted."

Angelicus' eyes grew true blue. "I should have known better. I shouldn't have judged."

"Anyway, Professor," added Zak, "past the city, there's lots more farms and pine forests. You'll like it."

The bubble glided higher through the polluted sky and out over a shipyard. There were hundreds of ships, big and small, all painted the same shade of gray.

"Look, Ivy, there's the navy yard. The one we visited on our class trip."

Angelicus cocked his head. "What do they do in a navy yard?"

"They build ships," answered Zak. "Warships."

The professor was shocked. "Warships? I thought they were extinct. What do they do with these warships?"

"Well, they take soldiers and planes and bombs and rockets around the world to keep the peace. They bomb the bad leaders and kill the terrorists—the enemies of peace," Zak explained.

"Let me get this straight." Angelicus scratched his lower left ear in disbelief. "You have warships that kill people and make war—to keep the peace? I'm afraid that doesn't make a whole lot of sense to me." His eyes grew dark, almost black. "War makes war. Peace makes peace."

"I'm glad you said that, Professor. Most of us kids feel that way too," said Ivy.

"Well, the Guardian Residents should listen to you children. How do they think the water feels about all this? This navy business must be very disruptive to the water."

While they were talking, the light had grown dimmer in the craft and everything outside took on a dark, murky haze.

The lights on the pipe grew brighter and the funny voice

sounded again. "Surface compromised. Surface compromised."

Angelicus turned to examine the pipe. "There's something forming on the skin of the bubble. Hmm . . . hydrocarbons."

"Down there, Professor—smoke!" yelled Ivy. She pointed to a flaming smokestack below them.

"That's an oil refinery," said Zak.

Ziggy looked down and snarled. That didn't smell like just smoke to him. He saw a greasy black bubble swirling in the menacing cloud, and it was definitely alive. It was spinning around and around, aiming the smoke and the flames directly at them. He growled another warning and bared his teeth.

"Ssh!" Angelicus commanded. His eyes turned a piercing yellow and with a subtle but firm shake of his head, he signaled the little dog to get away from the edge.

Ziggy shrank back, trying to ignore what he had just seen. He was confused and hurt that the professor didn't heed his warning.

Angelicus turned to Zak as if nothing had gone on between him and Ziggy.

"Oil refinery?" he asked.

Ivy and Zak had missed the interchange between Ziggy and the professor.

"Yeah. To make fuel—for power," said Zak.

"Power? What's wrong with the sun? The wind? The water? They have enough power to share with you. On Quantia we simply store up little bits of lightning from time to time. Everything is inside out around here. That oil belongs inside the Earth. Your Guardian Residents better put on their thinking caps!"

His ears drooped, his eyes grew smoky gray, and an indescribably sad look crossed his face. "Oh dear, oh dear. This just won't do."

"Don't be sad, Professor," said Ivy, "when I grow up I'm gonna be a scientist. I'm gonna figure out how to clean everything up."

"Yeah, Professor," Zak added, "we're gonna take care of the Earth."

Suddenly a great roar was heard in the distance.

"What's that!" yelled Angelicus.

Ziggy growled.

"It's a jet, Professor," responded Zak.

By this time nothing could be seen through the gloom of the refinery exhaust that had blackened the bubble. The noise grew closer and louder till it reached deafening proportions. Ziggy howled and Angelicus pushed furiously on the controls.

"Whatever that noisy contraption is, we'd better get out of the way," he said. "Hold onto your chairs!"

The jet blasted by, narrowly missing them, but the bubble got caught in its slipstream. Thrown into a terrible spin and out of control, it headed blindly toward the flaming exhaust stack. The children screamed as the bubble careered downward.

Zak and Ivy reached out for each other, trying desperately to stabilize themselves against the mighty forces of the spin. Ziggy wailed. Ivy tried to grab him but he kept slipping from her grasp.

Zak called out, "Professor, what'll we do? Can't you stop it?"

Angelicus' voice was strangely calm amid the turmoil. "I'm afraid we'll just have to leave it to the forces of nature," he said quietly.

"What?" Zak yelled. He peered over toward the professor, who was braced firmly against the bubble's wall, his eyes closed in deep concentration.

Zak turned to Ivy, but as he started to speak, they felt a soft bump, then a gentle bounce and a change in the bubble's direction. It was as if they had landed on a hill of marshmallows or soft feather pillows.

"Professor . . ." started Ivy, but was interrupted.

"Ah," called out Angelicus into the air, "I thought you might hear me. And just in time, I might add."

The children were stunned when another voice spoke from outside the craft. With a croak, it said, "I told you we'd be around, Professor."

"That's the turkey buzzard!" yelled Ivy, excited.

"We could see you were in trouble from a distance, but we didn't know if we could catch you. Me 'n Ralph had to put our wings together. We each took a side. Half on his wing, half on mine," called out the buzzard. "You gotta be careful around here. You can get your feathers singed real bad if you don't keep your eyes open. We don't even come down here anymore."

"Well, I'm certainly glad you made an exception this time," returned Angelicus. "Is there someplace you can set us down? We'll have to blow a new bubble, or we'll never get down to the bay."

"No problem. We'll set you down on the riverbank."

The other buzzard called out, "Hey Mikey! Look down, over there. Them mounds of dirt by the river."

"Yeah, Ralph. That looks good. Let's try it."

The buzzards glided downward, gingerly balancing the blackened bubble between them. They swiftly lost altitude and, with a jolt, the bubble was safely back on land.

"Cover your eyes," yelled Angelicus, and grabbed a hold of the pipe.

No sooner had the children gotten their hands to their faces, the bubble popped. They felt a fine spray engulf them from head to toe.

"You can open your eyes now."

They dropped their hands and stood there, startled and dripping wet in the smoky haze of the city. Beneath their feet was a monstrous berm of lifeless soil. Rumbling iron bridges and freeways towered overhead.

Angelicus shook a few drops of sludgy water from the pipe. As he placed it in his belt, the buckle emitted a dim gray glow and a sound like thundering static. The startled buzzards jumped into the air.

"It's all right, boys," he said. "I know it's a little noisy. I've got to get that volume control adjusted one of these days."

Ivy took a look at her traveling companions. Their faces were smudged and streaked with soot and grime. "We're all dirty," she gasped. "And look at Ziggy."

Ziggy had turned from white and black to mucky gray and was furiously trying to lick himself clean.

Zak rubbed his eyes. "What a mess!" he said.

Mikey ruffled his feathers and spread out his greasy wings.

Ralph shook himself and took a clumsy hop forward. "Whew! That raw sewage even gets my attention. Almost makes ya want to throw up," he said.

"It's a pity what's happened to the city," agreed Mikey with a grunt.

"There's no mention of any of this in the *Planetary Guide*," returned Angelicus. "How do we get to the river?" He peered down at the river's edge. A brick wall separated the water from the trees and earth. "And what's this we're standing on?"

"This is river bottom, Professor, if you get my drift," answered Mikey. "They dig it out to make a channel for the ships. They use some of it to fill in small streams and the marshlands."

Angelicus' ears twitched and his flower antenna wilted. "Oh my!" he exclaimed. "Where does the river go in the flood times? It must get awfully worked up! Anyway, even if we could climb down this wall, I couldn't get a bubble going from that water. Almost all of its sparkle is gone."

Ivy turned to Zak. "We've gotta do something."

"Don't worry," Zak said hopefully, "we'll find pure water. We'll figure something out. Won't we, Professor?"

Angelicus looked doubtful.

An orange and black butterfly had been flying along the base of the berm and, overhearing their conversation, flew up to the group. "Zis truly eez a mess, Professeur." The butterfly spoke in a faint, accented voice. "Forgive me, I could not help but hear. Permit me to introduce myself. I am ze Countess Monique ze Monarch. Perhaps I can be of some assistance. I know zis area well. I am on my way to a wonderful garden. Ze vegetables and flowers are crazy about ze water zere! I can take you."

"Are you French?" asked Ivy, recognizing the insect's accent.

"Oo! You noticed. How nice," replied the butterfly.

Before Ivy could respond that she'd met a French exchange student at school, Mikey spoke up.

"Well, Professor," he said, "it looks like you're in good hands. We gotta get back upriver. When you get down to the bay, make sure you look up our cousin, Water Eagle."

"Well, thanks for everything, boys. Have a safe flight," said Angelicus.

The buzzards turned to leave. They stumbled a few steps and hopped. Then, with a quick push of their fleshy legs and visibly straining their great wings, they finally got under way. When they were airborne, they turned back for one last circle over the travelers.

"Catch ya later, Professor," Mikey called out.

The children and Angelicus called out their thanks again as the raptors smoothly moved up and out of sight.

"Well," said Monique, "zey certainly aren't ze most graceful, are zey?" She fanned herself with one wing.

"Hey—they saved our life!" said Zak, insulted.

Monique quickly corrected herself: "Oo, but good souls. Oui, oui—good souls."

Angelicus didn't notice their interchange. "What was this about a garden?" he asked.

"Oui, oui. Lovely, glorieuse. Magnifique! Absolutely overflowing wiz pollen. Sometimes I must peench myself." The butterfly's big iridescent eyes glowed with anticipation. "I really must be going," she said, and fluttered off.

"Wait," yelled Ivy, "aren't you going to show us?"

Monique stopped short and turned back toward them. "Ah, oui. How absolutely thoughtless! Of course, by all means. Well . . . come along."

She turned again and headed down the berm with Angelicus, Ziggy, and the children scrambling behind her.

"Eet eez not far," she called out in her musical voice.

THE GARDENS

The children, Angelicus, and Ziggy followed Monique along a winding, rutted lane. Huge mounds of lifeless, gray dirt formed a canyon on either side of them. They passed a dump under a concrete bridge and unexpectedly saw black-eyed-susans growing there among the debris. Pink morning glories and Queen Anne's lace dotted the walls of river bottom along the pathway.

Monique slowed at a bunch of wild daisies. "Pardon me, but I am very thirsty," she said, and lighted on a large blossom to drink. "Oo, zat was sooo delightful," she exclaimed, and with a quick flutter of her wings, continued on. "Well, come on, zen. Come along."

They crossed over a railroad track, turned a corner and came upon the rusted hulk of an abandoned asphalt plant. Posted on a chainlink fence surrounding the plant a country sign read Pure Honey For Sale. The letters were hand painted black and an arrow pointed toward a partially hidden lane.

"Ah," said Angelicus, his eyes lighting up to a bright blue, "honey. Bee Sharelings. They must have a hive here."

"And if there're bees, there're flowers!" exclaimed Ivy.

"Yeah," said Zak, "and water."

"What do you s'ink I 'ave been zaying?" asked Monique petulantly. "Would I not tell you zee truth?"

Ziggy raced ahead.

"Wait for us, Ziggy," the children yelled, and ran after him.

A group of monarchs flew by Monique and Angelicus, waving "hello" as they passed.

"Bonjour," she called out.

Along the lane was a tall patchwork fence made of old doors, rusty metal mesh, and sheets of red, blue and yellow painted plywood. Grapevines and giant squashes were climbing all over it.

The children pulled back some of the vines and peered through the fence. They saw apple, peach and fig trees, beanpoles, cornstalks, tomatoes and peppers. A rabbit poked his head out from between a pumpkin and a giant cabbage. Zinnias, orange and yellow marigolds, red canna lilies and gladiolus of every color stood up straight like a choir of trumpets calling out to their friends, the bees and butterflies, to share their sweet nectars. The sound of birds chirping and singing, honeybees buzzing and hundreds of butterflies fluttering their wings filled the air.

"Professor! Hurry! Come look!" shouted Ivy.

Angelicus and Monique caught up to the children, the professor's eyes dazzling brilliant aquamarine at the magical sight.

"What a wonderful garden!" he exclaimed.

Ziggy was jumping up and down, trying to catch butterflies, and running around in circles like a puppy.

"I've never seen so many butterflies before," said Ivy.

"Can you believe it?" said Zak. He pointed back toward the lifeless mounds and highways looming beyond the trees. "All these flowers right here in the middle of the city!"

"Eet ees all in ze nature of things," intoned Monique. "Before ze humans planted zese gardens, we had nowhere to stop for miles and miles. But now zis ees one of our favorite spots. We always come here on our way south. Oo—perfumes! Zey are exquisite!" She fluttered up and out of sight over the fence.

The others walked on till they came to a gate, partially ajar. Zak poked his head in and saw an older man with long salt-and-pepper hair pulled back in a ponytail. He was sitting in front of a silver-painted shack made out of the recycled rear end of a school bus. Clusters of braided red and white onions, garlic and herbs were hung to dry from a makeshift awning over a bright blue plywood door. The man was surrounded by a large group of small white cats with black spots. He was talking with each one as he fed them.

"Excuse me, sir," Zak called out, "do you think you can help us? We need water."

The man looked up at the strange, grimy travelers. His eyes opened wide. "I guess you do, man!" He chuckled and said, "What happened to your friend here—he get lost on a Halloween trip?"

"Oh, this is Professor Angelicus. He's from another planet and he needs to get home."

Ivy rushed in. "Yeah, for the Rainbow Festival. So we need clean water for his bubble pipe and the river's too dirty, so we have to get down to the bay."

"Whoa! Another planet, eh? Hey, that's cool, man. I been there." The gardener smiled and winked knowingly. "What planet, Venus? I mean—them ears, man. Too much!"

"No, I come from Quantia," Angelicus said seriously. "Do you know it?"

"Ah . . . Quantia. Can't say I do. But, hey, whatever does it for you. I do have clean water here. You're welcome to it." He picked up a gallon bottle of spring water. "I just bought it this morning."

Angelicus was shocked. "You buy your water to feed all these vegetables and flowers?"

The man laughed again. "Nah, man!" he exclaimed. "There's plenty of groundwater here for the flowers. I pump it up by hand." He pointed to an old-fashioned red hand pump mounted over an old clawfoot bathtub. "But I don't feel cool drinking it. I used to go trout fishing up in the mountains and we could take water for coffee right out of the stream. But you just can't do that anymore. If you want to wash up, just use the pump. That water's fine for that."

The children and Angelicus gathered around the tub and began to wash themselves off.

Ziggy was rolling around on the ground, scratching his back. The cats came over to him and started to help, purring and licking him clean.

"Geez, you have a lot of cats," Ivy remarked.

"They ain't really mine. They just live here in the gardens," the man responded. "It all started with ol' Suzie Green Eyes, there. Years ago."

He pointed to an ancient cat stretched out, bathing in the sunlight by the shack. She looked up wisely and yawned.

"Someone dropped her off here all fat with kittens. I guess they couldn't feed any more cats. Anyway, soon there were six more and then twelve and then . . ." He spread his arms out and shrugged. "Somebody's gotta feed 'em, so I come every day."

The professor smiled. "That's very sharing of you," he said. "These are extraordinary gardens—so happy and full of life. Who planted them? How did this happen?"

The gardener answered, "Did you see that old farmhouse on the other side of the road? When the oil company bought up this land years ago, the old beekeeper there wouldn't sell out, so they didn't have enough room to put a refinery. A bunch of us who worked for 'em told our friends and we just sorta squatted here. We don't have room where we live in the city to grow fresh vegetables and flowers, so this was perfect. They don't bug us about it. We been here about twenty years now."

"And we are sooo glad you are!" exclaimed Monique. She and a few of her friends had been gathered around a trumpet vine growing up the side of a garden shed and she flew over to the group, landing on the gardener's shoulder. "You've brought back ze wildflowers. They're absolutely delectable!"

"It warms my heart to see some Guardian Residents remembering the Shareling ways and helping restore the natural order of your Big Blue Ball." Angelicus' eyes turned a deep forest green and the antenna on his head opened like an exotic tulip, slowly revolving in all directions as if absorbing the energies of the glorious gardens. "Well, we must be going," he said with a start. "I think the water from your pump will do just fine for our needs." He removed the pipe from his belt.

"Whoa, man," said the gardener, "can I take a look at that?"

Angelicus smiled and held out the pipe. The gardener looked closely.

"Man! I used to have a pipe something like this—but I didn't use it for blowin' bubbles, if you know what I mean! I got rid of it years ago, though, when I found out how bad smoking is for you." He began pumping the water.

Angelicus placed the pipe under the spigot. The stream of water splashed from the bowl as it filled, shimmering and glimmering in the sunlight. "Yes," he repeated with a grin, "I think this will do just fine. It certainly has enough sparkle for a bubble to take us to the bay."

"OK, kids," he continued, "let's get ready. Thank you so much for your help, sir."

The children came close to the professor. Zak bent down to pick up Ziggy and Ziggy licked him on the face.

"Yuck!" yelled Zak, and held the dog away from him. "Your breath smells awful! You were eating cat food!"

Ziggy wagged his tail.

It suddenly dawned on the gardener that this had all been for real. "You weren't trippin' me, were you? You're gonna travel in a bubble—you really are from another planet!"

"Of course," said Angelicus. "We'd love to stay and learn more about your gardens but we really have to be going."

"How does that pipe thing work, anyway?" asked the astounded gardener.

"It's simple. Just watch."

Monique fluttered around the little group as Angelicus fiddled with the controls on the pipe.

"Perhaps we will meet again soon," she sang out. "My friends and I are heading in the same direction. We're crazy about ze meadows by ze bay!"

The gardener watched in amazement as Angelicus blew on the pipe. An iridescent stream quickly surrounded the foursome and the bubble slowly started rising.

"Thank you for all your help," called out Zak and Ivy.

Monique fluttered her wings. "Bon voyage!"

Ziggy barked and wagged his tail.

Suzie Green Eyes affectionately rubbed up against the gardener's leg. He picked her up and petted her on the head as he raised his fingers in a "V."

"Peace!" he called out, and stepped back as the bubble started spinning. The cats looked up as the birds sang. The flowers turned to watch. A breeze filled the air and the trees swayed. The rainbow colors raced across the surface of the bubble as it floated high into the air.

"We'd better get moving," Angelicus said.

"Yeah, Professor. I just remembered. I've got to get home in time for dinner," Zak said anxiously.

"Don't worry, Zak. You'll be home in time."

Angelicus adjusted the controls on the pipe. The lights blinked . . . red, blue and purple. A look of intense concentration came over his face and the children watched as his eyes changed again. They were like clear glass marbles sparkling in the afternoon sun.

The pipe spoke up: "Speed adjusted. Temporal compensation complete. Moving in and out of time . . . in and out of time."

Zak glanced at his watch. The dial was spinning crazily . . . . first forward, then backward, and then finally it just stopped. The wind howled as it came from the north and swept the bubble up and sent it rushing through the turquoise summer sky, whizzing and tumbling through white fluffy clouds. The bubble spun faster and faster, higher and higher, and the light outside grew dimmer as they felt a distinct change of forces. Rather than being pushed by the wind, it felt as if some supernatural force was pulling them from above—as if they were being swallowed up by an enormous tornado.

Ivy called out, "What's happening, Professor?"

The professor's voice sounded as if it were miles away. "It's just the Great Universal Source assisting us."

Everything became very black and all movement stopped completely. They were floating free. The darkness was more than a lack of light . . . it was a warm, dense, rich silent blackness unlike anything the children had ever known before. It wasn't frightening; they felt tranquil and pleasantly calm, rather like the alignment they'd experienced earlier. In the total blackness the professor radiated a soft white light.

"Ivy," exclaimed Zak, "look, we're glowing too—and so is Ziggy!"

"Yeah, Zak, we're glowing just like angels," responded Ivy.

The professor chuckled. "Now hold steady," he said.

The next thing they knew the bubble was floating, rocking like a ball in the gentle swell of the bay, and they were brilliantly bathed in the silvery luminescence of a full moon. They could hear the quiet, rhythmic lapping of the tide against the shore.

THE BAY, KING HARRY, AND THE SHOREBIRDS

"Beep, beep-beep, beep, beep, beep-beep ..." Ziggy put his paws over his ears and the professor's antenna rotated nervously.

"Beep, beep ... beep ..."

"What is that incessant noise?" Angelicus demanded. "Who is signaling us?"

"I don't hear anything, Professor," said Zak.

"Listen," said Ivy. "Hear it? That real quiet beeping?"

"Quiet? That sound is positively deafening!" Angelicus roared, and his upper ears slammed shut.

Ziggy barked in agreement.

"Well, what do you think it is?" Ivy asked.

"Look!" Zak pointed. "It's a sea turtle."

In the moonlit bay a large turtle had appeared by the side of the bubble. Through the invisible wall they watched as it slowly stretched its wrinkled neck clear of the water. The skin around its eyes was marked like a giraffe and its long neck disappeared into a mahogany colored, leathery shell.

"It's a loggerhead!" exclaimed Ivy. (She always got an A in science.) "But look at its back. What's that—on its shell—those little black boxes?"

"They look like transmitters," Zak said. "Like the ones they put in weather balloons."

The turtle blinked its eyes, then spoke up. "You're Professor Angelicus, aren't you?" it said. "I'm Tantra. The birds told me you were on your way here."

"How do you do," said Angelicus. "Is that noise coming from those boxes?"

"Yes, it is," the turtle responded. "I got caught in the intake pipes of a nuclear power plant up the bay. I could have drowned, but the humans were kind enough to save me. After they rescued me, they put these beeping boxes on my shell. They've been dying to know where we loggerheads go . . . our natural paths, and about our lifestyle. They can follow me by listening to the box from satellites. If you think it hurts your ears, imagine what it does to mine!"

"Well, let me give you a hand with that."

The professor removed the pipe from the inside of the bubble, pushed a button, and the pipe instantly turned into a wide, flat screwdriver. He slipped it through the skin of the bubble and inserted the tool under the edge of one of the boxes.

"You won't feel a thing," he promised. "I'll have that gadget off in no time." With a quick twist, Angelicus pried the box clear of the turtle's shell, and then repeated the operation on the other box. He reached through with his other hand to grab them, but they slid into the water.

"Oh dear," he said, "the beeping has stopped but now we've put those things into the water!"

"I wouldn't worry too much, Professor," said Tantra. "If you saw the junk at the bottom of this bay, you wouldn't even think twice about those things. And boy, I sure feel a lot more comfortable. Is there anything I can do for you in return?" The turtle bobbed up and down in the water.

"Well, I'm trying to get home to Quantia. Zak, Ivy and Ziggy, here, have been nice enough to help me. And the *Planetary Guide* says your Big Blue Ball has the perfect water to fuel my pipe. We were hoping—"

"Yeah, I know," Tantra interrupted, "the water's not the way it used to be. Certainly not in this bay." He thought a moment. "You know who might be able to help you? The horseshoe crabs. They get around. They've been taking the same path here for five hundred million years."

Ivy was stunned. "The horseshoe crabs were here before the dinosaurs?" she asked.

"Well, sure," said the turtle. "They're about the oldest folks on Earth. They come here in the spring when the sun, the moon and the Earth align. They follow the clock of the Earth." He looked up at the full moon. "They're all probably on the beach by now. The tide has turned."

"It's spring again, Ivy!" exclaimed Zak. "In the city it was summer. This is extremely excellent!"

Angelicus grinned. "That's Bubble Time, Zak. We just changed seasons. Today we're in yesterday. Yesterday might be tomorrow."

Angelicus and the children bid farewell to Tantra and wished him a safe voyage. A westerly sea breeze blew across the bay and the bubble drifted toward the shore. Moonbeams reflected on the waves. They could smell the salt in the air. Minnows and small crabs swam gracefully beneath the surface of the shallow water, shimmering in the soft light, phosphorescence in their wake spreading out like angel wings around them.

As they approached the beach, Angelicus said to the children, "Just in case the pipe doesn't accept this water, I'd better save this bubble. So be ready to jump."

Just before the bubble touched the sandy shore he pushed two buttons and the pipe played a little melody. The bubble instantly shrank and, with a loud SLURP, shriveled up back into the bowl. The children weren't prepared for the change and they rolled out onto the beach. Ziggy jumped out and barked at the breaking waves.

"Hey! Watch where you're going!" a voice hollered out from beneath Zak.

Zak jumped up and saw the outline of two horseshoe crabs on the sand. Their bodies were half-moon shaped, and they had long spiked tails. One was much larger than the other—about twice its size. The voice had come from the smaller of the two.

"Eek!" shrieked Ivy. "Look out, Zak, they're everywhere!"

Zak turned and, sure enough, the beach was literally covered with the prehistoric-looking creatures. Like army tanks, they were ponderously moving across the moonlit sand by the hundreds. The children could hear the sound of the crabs' shells scraping and clattering as they clambered over each other.

"Excuse me," Zak said, "I'm sorry. I didn't mean to fall on you."

"It really wasn't his fault," interjected Angelicus. "My friends aren't used to traveling in a bubble. I guess I was a little abrupt in my landing. Tantra, the turtle, said you might be able to help us. I'm Professor Angelicus."

"Oh, that's OK," answered the crab. His two eyes, set wide apart on the top of his olive brown shell, glimmered as he spoke. "I should have been watching. I've got nine eyes, you know. But I was a little preoccupied with Lady Anne, here. She dragged me over to fertilize her eggs."

"Oooh, Harry, darlin'," the large female protested in a saccharin-sweet, southern belle voice. "I didn't drag you. I chose you first. You see how many suitors I have, Professor."

A large group of males surrounded her. She poked a large claw out from under her shell at one of them. It came scuttling toward her.

Harry's rugged voice spoke up again. "I'm called Harry. King Harry."

Ivy asked, "Are you a king? King of the horseshoe crabs?"

The crab chuckled. "Naw," he said, "I'm no king. They call us king crabs. Never could figure that out. We sure aren't the biggest. Maybe it's because we're the oldest." He chuckled again. "Or maybe it's because we have blue blood."

He stopped and thought for a minute, then slowly turned toward the professor. "Did you say your name was Professor Angelicus? That name rings a bell. Hmm . . . you're not the fella who wrote that guidebook, are you? You know, the one about traveling through the universe and to the planets?"

The professor laughed. "No, that was my grandfather, Hortus. You sure have a long memory. He wrote the *Planetary Guide* thousands of years ago."

"Well," answered the crab with a wag of his long, spiked tail, "we remember the ancient Shareling ways. We pass them down from generation to generation. Anyway, you said you need help. What can I do for you?"

"I've got to find pure water or I'll never get home to Quantia," answered Angelicus. "My pipe can't blow a strong enough bubble unless I spark it with absolutely pure, clean water."

"Hmm," returned the crab. "That can be a problem anymore. Some of us have gotten used to the water. But it's true. It has changed." He paused again.

"Well," he continued, "soon it'll be daybreak, and the shorebirds will be arriving from the south. They feed on our leftover eggs. I've missed the tide going out and have a twelve-hour wait before it comes back in, so I have time to introduce you around. Some of the birds fly thousands of miles. They come from as far away as the great rain forest. They go north after they stop here and they really see a lot. Maybe they'll know."

He shifted in the sand a little and went on. "But if they can't help, you know who might be able to? Serena. The dolphin. I just saw her down at the mouth of the bay playing with her calves. She's real smart . . . and I'll tell you, she doesn't miss a trick. Yeah, she'll probably know something. I'd check with her."

The sun was rising over the meadow, bathing the tips of the tall sea grasses with a soft peach and lavender glow. The colors shimmered in the still water of the marsh pools and the majestic white egrets were moving gracefully through the reeds. On the beach thousands of various little shorebirds were landing . . . red knots, sandpipers and turnstones.

The musical cheeping and piping of the shorebirds, mixed with the raucous cries of the laughing gulls, the whistles of the terns and the grunts of the herring gulls, created a glorious racket.

Two stiff-tailed, ruddy ducks were courting on the bay. The blue-billed male made a drumming sound in his throat and flapped his wings to create a magic show of bubbles on the surface of the water for his female friend.

"Wow," yelled Zak over the din, "look at that! And that!" He pointed to the horizon.

A cloud of sanderlings flew in low over the bay and turned down the beach with breathtaking precision. The sunlight reflected off the white under their wings and sparkled against the water. Thousands upon thousands of birds zigzagged in graceful formations across the morning sky. A flock of snow geese formed a ragged "V" against the pink clouds as they flew overhead on their way north. As one leader grew tired of creating the draft for his fellow travelers he fell back and was immediately replaced by another.

Angelicus looked around with a wide grin on his face. His aquamarine eyes were brilliantly shining. "This is swell," he said. "What a wonderful celebration of life! A Shareling feast day if I've ever seen one."

"Feast is right," affirmed Harry with a muffled voice. He was digging himself into the sand to keep moist while waiting for the next tide to arrive. "The birds eat about three hundred tons of our eggs every year," he said as he disappeared under the sand.

Ivy looked at the tiny, transparent green eggs covering the beach, and did some quick calculations. "They must eat trillions and trillions of them!" she exclaimed.

A loud, shrieking howl interrupted their discussion.

"That sounds like Ziggy!" cried out Zak.

"Yeah, where is he?" answered Ivy.

CHAPTER NINE

The children looked around and Ziggy was nowhere in sight.

"Come on," yelled Zak, his heart pounding.

They all ran toward the marsh, in the direction of Ziggy's piercing cry.

BORRELL THE IMPOSTER

The children raced down a lane paved with crushed shells and came upon a sign reading SLOW DOWN—TURTLE CROSSING. A diamondback terrapin was pulling himself across the road, toward the bay.

"Have you seen a little dog?" Zak breathlessly asked the turtle.

Lethargically, the turtle looked up at them. He asked slowly, "A white and black one?"

"Yes, yes," answered Zak.

"Ah. Yes. Back there. In the marsh." The reptile pointed. "A little dog is being attacked by a giant tick. Awful sight," he said, and lazily continued across the road.

Angelicus came puffing up behind the children. "What's going on?" he asked.

"It's Ziggy," yelled Ivy, "he's in trouble!"

They looked in the direction the turtle had pointed and saw an angry flock of red-winged blackbirds swooping down and yelling at something hidden in the tall grass.

"He must be there," Ivy said, panting.

They all ran off toward the birds. Zak got there first and, pushing his way through the reeds, saw a scene that made his heart stop. Just as the turtle had said, poor Ziggy was in a death grip with a giant tick!

"Oh my stars!" exclaimed Angelicus. "It's Borrell. Borrell the Imposter!"

"This is a nightmare," screamed Ivy.

"Nightmare is right! That's exactly what it is, Ivy. A bad dream," said Angelicus. "Imagination gone haywire."

"I've got to save him!" yelled Zak, and he started toward Ziggy.

"No, Zak!" shrieked Ivy. "Professor!" She dove and tackled Zak before he reached the flattened grasses of the battleground. "Professor," she repeated, "do something!"

Angelicus reached his hand out and helped the children up. "Don't lose control," he said to Zak with compassion in his voice. His eyes turned a soft, pale turquoise. "Stay centered. Borrell is a parasite who feeds off of fear—a monstrous demon who takes the shape of your worst nightmare. He moves into the pockets of negative energy and changes into whatever you fear the most.

"The best thing you can do," Angelicus said, "is to stay calm and think positive. Call upon your Guardian Angels to help. In your mind's eye, picture the things you love the most . . . beautiful flowers . . . the warmth of the family. Loving feelings drive

Borrell away like hot peppers chase a puppy. Just close your eyes, align yourself, and think only good thoughts. Borrell can't stand good thoughts."

Zak and Ivy tightly closed their eyes. Zak's hands were clenched and he was focusing with all his might.

But Ivy, as hard as she tried, couldn't get control of her emotions. She opened her eyes wide and screamed at what she saw. "Professor, Zak—look what's happening!"

The giant tick was changing shape. Fire and lightning were shooting from the tick's mouth and black smoke was billowing from huge warts that were growing on its back.

"That's it. You've got Borrell on the run now," Angelicus said. "Keep it up, Zak."

"What do you mean?" asked Ivy. "It's awful . . . it's worse than before. It looks like it's turning into an oil refinery or something. That monster's going to burn Ziggy up, Professor!"

"The imposter's trying other shapes . . . it knows you're on to it. It can become almost anything," the professor breathlessly answered.

They all watched as Ziggy broke free from the demon's grasping pincers and wiped the black soot from his eyes. He let out a rumbling growl and fearlessly reentered the battle. Round and around they went in a blur of flames, fur and smoke.

"Go, Ziggy, go!" yelled Zak, concentrating even harder. He pictured the creek path and the sun sparkling on the waterfall from the old canal. He saw his favorite willow tree weeping out over the river.

Again the monstrous tick changed shape: it let out a thunderous roar and its body metamorphosed into a long, scaly, fire-breathing serpent with a venomous tongue darting in and out of its mouth. It got a hold on Ziggy's hind legs with the tip of its tail and began to coil itself around the little dog, twisting and flipping on the ground.

"Ivy, help!" Zak yelled.

Ivy closed her eyes and with all her heart and soul, began to concentrate, praying for Ziggy to be all right. Her mother's beautiful flower garden crossed her line of vision . . . and her favorite doll. She felt the coziness of her lacy bedroom at home.

"Good thoughts, Ivy. Beautiful thinking," intoned Angelicus. "That's it, Zak. See? Look, you're getting to Borrell now."

The vile serpent started shrinking. Its gargantuan head and awesome scaly body changed into a common viper, then to a plain, ordinary garden snake.

Zak yelled, "Look, it's shedding its skin!"

It continued going through changes and, within just a few seconds, the terrifying creature had become nothing more than a short, slimy, wriggling eel.

Ivy's face scrunched up and she said, "Ooh, gross! Yuck!"

Panting and shaking, Ziggy raced to jump into Zak's arms.

"Are you all right, Ziggy?" asked Zak. With a sigh of relief, he stroked his dog on the head.

Ziggy wagged his tail, then growled again at the eel writhing on the ground. It was still spitting little flares of sparks from its mouth.

A loud, melodic "KREE" was heard echoing across the marsh, and they looked up to see a giant raptor swooping low toward the scene of the battle. The bird's bright yellow eyes stood out against the black mask that wrapped around its white head. Its large golden brown wings were swept back and its green and white feet were stretched forward.

"It's an osprey!" yelled Zak.

The professor said, "Ah, Water Eagle. Ralph and Mikey's cousin."

The osprey called out and plunged feet first, grabbing the slimy creature in its sharp claws. With a powerful beating of its wings, the bird carried its prey high out over the bay. The children, Ziggy, and Angelicus ran toward the beach to watch.

"What's the osprey going to do?" asked Ivy.

"We'll see," answered Angelicus.

Soon enough, the magnificent sea eagle came to a halt in midair. Fluttering its wings furiously and with a ruffle of its feathers, it dropped the creature. Down and down, twisting and turning in the air and sputtering sparks from its mouth, the eel plunged toward the bay.

The eel hit the water and quickly turned into a worm. As it skimmed across the surface, flames streaked across the bay. Then, in a cloud of steam, the demon sizzled and disappeared from sight under the gentle waves.

A crowd of shorebirds and gulls had joined the spectators on the beach. They all cheered as the osprey headed back from his rescue mission.

"Thank you, Water Eagle!" yelled out Zak as the bird swooped overhead.

Ziggy yipped and wagged his tail furiously in gratitude.

"Happy to be of help," called down the raptor as he circled over their heads and headed back over the marsh.

"I guess he's your Guardian Angel, Ziggy," said Ivy. She patted him on the head.

"Hey," said Zak, "where's Harry? And Lady Anne?"

"Yeah, where are they?" added Ivy. "I don't see any horseshoe crabs anywhere on the beach."

The birds and gulls started yelling and squawking at once.

"Whoa, whoa, whoa," said Angelicus. "You can't all talk at once. One at a time! Or I won't be able to hear any of you."

"Professor," croaked out one of the laughing gulls, "two humans came and loaded them all into a big truck. I think they were poachers. I heard them saying they're gonna trade them for something called money."

"What does that mean?" asked Angelicus. "Why would they do that?"

A sandpiper piped up. "I heard them talking. They said they can get money for the crabs' blue blood—for research—and they can sell them for bait and fertilizer."

"They're not supposed to do that," chirped the tern. "Years ago, the red humans only used their discarded tails for arrowheads. They respected the crabs and the Earth. They only took what they needed."

"Now we won't have any eggs to eat," peeped a sanderling.

"I've got five thousand miles to fly before I can eat again," squeaked a red knot angrily. "I need to double my body weight. I need those eggs!"

"Those men are taking more than they need," intoned an egret. "Even the humans post signs not to touch the crabs during mating season."

"Oh," sighed Ivy, "those poor crabs. All piled up in the back of a truck. Without water."

Zak said, "They're not being Sharelings, are they, Professor?"

"Certainly not!" snapped Angelicus. "This just won't do!"

Ziggy watched the professor's eyes flare to a cardinal red. "Oh no," the little dog thought, "it's just like my friends told me. The humans are taking more than they need."

"We've got to save them, Professor!" yelled Ivy.

"It's a good thing I saved that bubble," said Angelicus. "We're going to stop that truck."

"We'll help you, Professor," the shorebirds called out. "We're going with you."

"Quick, kids, get ready for a bumpy ride." The professor pulled the pipe from his belt and pushed on the red button.

"Emergency startup. Emergency startup," called out the pipe.

The buckle let out a clap of thunder and, with one brilliant burst of light, the children, Ziggy, and Angelicus were in the bubble.

"Which way did they go?" called out the professor.

"South," answered the birds. "We'll show you."

With a determined look on his face, Angelicus pulled back on the controls and the craft instantly shot into the air. Thousands of shorebirds filled the sky. They surrounded the bubble like a military squadron prepared to escort the children and Angelicus down the bay.

The shiny bubble and cloud of birds streaked south across the sky like thunder and lightning before a summer storm, heading along the shore road.

THE DOLPHINS, THE NET, AND SEETASHA THE WHALE

"Hey, Andy, look at all them birds! Look—there's thousands of 'em."

The passenger took a swig from a can of beer as the rusty old dump truck, filled to the brim with horseshoe crabs, rattled along the bay shore road. There were so many birds in the sky, they were blocking the sun.

Andy, the driver, exclaimed, "Holy cow, it's gettin' dark! What the heck is goin' on? I can't see the sky."

"Maybe a storm is comin'," said his partner. "We better get outta here."

From the bubble, Angelicus and the children looked down at the rocketing truck. The professor pushed the yellow button on the pipe to match their increasing speed.

Ivy asked, "Professor, don't you think you should slow down?"

"Stop being a backseat driver, Ivy. This is awesome," said Zak.

"We're speeding in Bubble Time," said Angelicus calmly. "We can't be hurt."

Ivy sat back in her rocking chair and tried to relax.

Zak yelled, "Professor, you've caught up to them!"

Ziggy jumped onto Zak's lap and barked down at the truck.

Angelicus adjusted the controls and the bubble started to spin. Red, purple, green and white light flashed across its surface. He shifted gears and they descended until the glowing craft was hovering over the truck.

"This should stop them, Professor," said Zak.

"Well, hopefully they'll see the light and pull over," said Angelicus.

But the poachers became more and more frightened.

"Hey, man, that's something from outer space—some kind of flying saucer. You better step on it! We gotta get outta here!"

"Aw, c'mon man," Andy said, "it's just your imagination. You've had one too many. Your eyes are trickin' you." But his hands were shaking on the steering wheel as he pushed farther down on the gas pedal and they sped on down the road.

"I guess we didn't get their attention," muttered Angelicus. He pushed even harder on the pipe. The dazzling, spinning bubble moved closer to the windshield of the truck.

"Holy Moses!" Andy yelled with terror in his voice. Blinded by the flashing light, he slammed on the brakes and cut the steering wheel hard to the right.

"Watch where you're going!" his buddy screamed.

But it was too late. The dump truck careered off the side of the road and crashed up onto a sand dune. It rocked back and forth for a minute, then finally rolled over on its side.

The two dazed poachers crawled out through the broken windshield of the truck and ran down the road yelling for their lives. A skunk ran out of the marsh, spraying his scent, and a flock of screaming seagulls and dive-bombing shorebirds chased after them.

Angelicus safely landed the bubble on the pebbly beach. The tide was coming in.

"Professor—under here!"

It was Harry's voice. He was calling out from under the hundreds of crabs that were slowly crawling out of the old truck, onto the sand.

As he worked his way free from the pile he continued: "How can we ever thank you, Professor Angelicus. We were goners for sure."

"Anytime, Harry. Happy to be of help."

"Well, Professor, me and my friends are gonna catch the high tide while it's here. But this is where the ocean meets the bay. This is where we saw Serena the dolphin yesterday. She's probably still here. I'm sure she can help you." Harry lumbered off toward the water. "Thanks again," he called out as he slipped beneath the waves.

"Hooray for Angelicus! Hooray! Hooray!" chanted the other crabs as, one by one, they headed into the ocean.

"Hooray!" sang out the shorebirds as they dispersed into the blue sky.

"Great teamwork, my friends," Angelicus answered.

"Look," yelled Ivy, "I think I see her. I think that's a dolphin over there."

A beautiful bottlenose dolphin was near the water's edge, playing with her calf.

"Serena, Serena," called out Zak and Ivy, running toward her.

"King Harry sent us," said Ivy.

"Yeah, he said you could help us find clean, pure water," said Zak.

"So that Professor Angelicus can get home to Quantia," finished Ivy.

"How do you do?" said the professor.

"Pleased to meet you," said the dolphin. She cocked her gray head up out of the water and looked straight at Angelicus. Her beautiful, compassionate eyes were shining as she moved her flippers slowly back and forth in the surf to keep herself stable.

A soft, gentle voice came from her white lips. "I honestly don't know what to tell you," she said. "Maybe if you go farther south and deeper into the ocean, you might find pure water. But the conditions here have gotten terrible, just terrible. We've been coming closer and closer trying to tell the humans that we need their help, but they're not listening. They just want to play with us. We like to play, but we need their help. We need them to clean up the water so my little Chakra, here, can grow up in a healthy environment."

The little dolphin nuzzled up close to its mother.

"Ooh," Ivy sighed, "isn't he cute, Zak?"

"Hi, Chakra. Nice to meet you," said Zak with a big smile on his face.

"Hi, Zak," answered the baby dolphin. "You wanna go swimming with me?"

"I can't now, Chakra. But some other time, for sure. I always wanted to swim with a dolphin," responded Zak.

"OK," said the little dolphin. He swam off to play in the nearby waves.

His mother called out, "Don't go too far!"

"I won't, Momma," he answered, and then dove beneath the waves. A minute later he popped back up with a bunch of dark green seaweed on his nose. He flipped it high into the air and raced to catch it.

The children laughed.

"That's a nice young fellow you've got there," said Angelicus softly, his eyes turning lavender blue. "It's a shame the Guardian Residents aren't listening."

"They're not all deaf," said Serena gently. "Some humans have been doing what they can . . . but there's so much to do! And so few helping! I understand how some of the good humans might lose faith sometimes."

"Hmm. There's a lot of hard work here. I can see how balancing this Big Blue Ball can be a very tricky business," agreed Angelicus sadly. His eyes got a faraway look and turned blue-gray as his upper ears drooped low over his forehead. "Oh dear, oh my falling stars!" he exclaimed. "Maybe I'll never get home for the Rainbow Festival."

"Aw, Professor, don't worry," said Zak, touching Angelicus' shoulder. "We'll find the water. You'll get home. I just know it."

Ivy took his hand. "You can't give up now. We'll find it. We'll find your water."

Ziggy barked and wagged his tail.

Angelicus looked at the children and smiled. His eyes were shining again, aquamarine.

Then all four of his green ears perked up, standing straight in the air and his flower antenna started rotating.

"I hear someone calling. I hear a whale Shareling," he said.

Little Chakra came racing over to his mother. "Momma, Momma," his voice rang out, "Aunt Seetasha's calling you. Dazzle's in trouble! He's caught in a fishing net."

"Oh no," said Serena in a worried voice. "I'm sorry, Professor, but I can't stay and chat. I've got to run. You know how inquisitive children can be. That older boy of mine is always getting into something. I've got to go to him."

"We understand, Serena," said Angelicus. "You go on ahead. We'll follow. Maybe we can help."

Serena and Chakra swam out over the waves and disappeared into the water, leaving a white wake behind them.

"Quick, kids," said Angelicus.

He surveyed the foaming, sunlit surf hitting the beach beneath their feet. The wind was blowing, the waves were breaking, and hundreds of little bubbles of seawater were bursting in the air and spraying their faces. The fragrance of the ocean filled their nostrils.

"I bet those bubbles will do just fine." He pulled out his pipe and scooped up one of the salty little bubbles into the bowl.

"You can fuel the pipe with one of those?" asked Ivy.

"Absolutely! Just watch."

He poked the bubble and it popped. The children watched it explode in slow motion.

"See that bubble power? Feel it? Hear it?" he asked. "It just split into two hundred and thirty-three drops of the richest, most nutritious water in the universe. It may not be pure enough to get me home to Quantia, but one of those little drops can take you anywhere on your Earth. After all, it's probably already been there once. It remembers! Each bubble feeds and fertilizes your Big Blue Ball. The tide of your sea is the clock—the rhythm—the life force of your planet. When the waves break, the water mixes with the air and millions of bubbles float to the surface. Each time a tiny bubble bursts, it shoots minerals and aquatic microorganisms into your air. Billion of tons of salt and millions of tons of organic matter evaporate into your Big Blue Ball's atmosphere every year."

"Yeah, Professor," Zak agreed, "that's how the Earth gets its food! From the raindrops."

"And that's how we get our fluffy white clouds," said Ivy, looking dreamily up at the sky.

"True and correct," said Angelicus with a smile. "You've certainly done your homework. Well, I guess we better stop talking. We need a bubble, not babble! Dazzle will be needing our help."

He bent down and scooped up another bubble from the sea, blew on the pipe, pushed a button, and the bubble grew around them. They lifted off into the afternoon sky.

The travelers zoomed out over the deep blue water. The whitecaps of the ocean sparkled as they raced along, following Serena and Chakra's wake.

"Look—up ahead!" yelled Zak. He pointed through the skin of the craft at the horizon.

An old blue and white fishing boat was bobbing in the swell, its crane bending from the weight of something it was trying to pull out of the sea.

"There's Serena," said Ivy.

Serena was circling frantically around the boat, with little Chakra by her side.

"That boat must be helping them," said Zak.

The bubble moved closer and hovered over an old fisherman on deck. He was struggling with the ancient boom.

"Hello down there," Angelicus called out, "need some help?"

The fisherman put his hand over his bushy eyebrows, his bright blue eyes squinting against the sun. "I don't know what you can do to help," he hollered back over the sound of the boat's motor. "There's a dolphin and some other fish all tangled up in an old net down there. It must be huge, 'cause my winch can't get it to budge. I'm worried about that dolphin. He could drown. They have to come up for air once in a while, y'know."

"Well, maybe we can be of assistance," responded the professor. "Can you keep your line steady?"

"Yeah, as long as I keep a little power up, the net will stay in place."

"OK," called out Angelicus.

"Professor, what're you gonna do?" asked Zak.

"Let's go down and find out what has to be done," Angelicus answered.

He gave a push on the controls and the pipe sang out: "Submarine mode. Preparing for underwater operation."

"Stay in your seats, kids," Angelicus warned.

The bubble spun like a top for a few seconds.

"Activation complete," the pipe announced.

They slipped into the cool, deep water.

"This is neat, Professor," said Ivy.

Ziggy jumped down from Zak's lap and pushed his nose to

the wall of the bubble, barking at the fish swimming by.

"Down there." Zak pointed at a cloud of bubbles rising up from a huge bundle of twisted rope and twine. "There's Dazzle!"

The young dolphin was hopelessly entangled in the net, squirming furiously and crying out.

Serena swam up to them. "Oh, those humans," she wailed, "when they don't have a use for something, they just dump it here in the ocean. Some of them don't think twice about it being our home! Oh, my Dazzle!"

"Why do they do that?" snorted Angelicus. "It's so inconsiderate!"

His eyes turned olive green. "What do they think the water can do with their garbage?"

"You ain't seen the half of it, Professor!" came a deep musical voice from behind them.

The children and Angelicus turned to see a huge eye peering in at them.

"Whoa!" yelled Zak and jumped back, bumping into Ivy.

The voice chuckled. "I wouldn't hurt you, little person. I'm Seetasha."

Ivy had been studying her and recognized the callous-like growths above the great mammal's eye. "Are you a right whale?" she asked.

"Right you are. And you folks are Professor Angelicus and friends, aren't you? You've come to help my little nephew."

"That's us," responded Angelicus. "It's nice to meet you, ma'am, but we'd better get on with this." He turned back to his controls as the bubble came to a stop near the fishing net.

"Professor, how are you going to do this?" asked Zak.

"Hmm. Let's see," said Angelicus. "I think I know. But I have to be very careful. Just stay steady, kids . . . don't rock the bubble, and we'll have this young whippersnapper out of here in a jiffy."

He maneuvered the bubble till it bumped up against the net, pulled the pipe free and tapped on the purple button three times. The pipe squawked and transformed into a long, skinny saw.

"Hold on there, Dazzle," said Angelicus.

With a quick thrust, he slipped the blade through the bubble's skin and, sawing away at the ropes, quickly freed the young dolphin from his prison.

Dazzle let out a loud whistle and raced toward the surface. Serena and Chakra followed and the three dolphins jumped for joy into the open air.

"Great job, Professor," said Zak, "you did it!"

After Angelicus returned the pipe to its normal position, it called out, "Rescue mission accomplished."

The craft started upwards toward the light. Thousands of other little bubbles surrounded them, rising up from the ocean floor.

"This is so cool," said Ivy. "Now I know how it feels to be the fizz in a glass of soda!"

Zak laughed and Ziggy barked as their bubble popped through the surface. Once again they were floating on the sea.

Serena was scolding Dazzle. "Thank goodness your Aunt Seetasha called me. And Professor Angelicus and the children were here to rescue you," she was blustering. "You've *got* to be more careful! You've got to watch where you're swimming!"

"Now," she continued, "you just thank the professor right now."

Bashfully, Dazzle swam over to the bubble. "Thank you, Professor Angelicus," he said meekly.

The professor smiled. "Don't just thank us. We could never have done it without this nice fisherman here." Angelicus looked up at the boat. "What is your name, sir? I'm Angelicus . . . Professor Angelicus of Quantia, and this is Zak, Ivy, and Ziggy."

"Pleased to meet you, Professor. I'm Peter—Peter the fisherman," the old man said. "And you don't have to thank me. The sea has given to me my whole life. The least I can do is give back a little."

Suddenly there was a giant splash. Seetasha the whale exuberantly burst through the waves. The sound of a fierce wind came from her two blowholes as a huge plume of water shot up toward the sun, spraying the bubble and the boat. A beautiful rainbow appeared in the whale's spray.

The fisherman was soaked and he reached for a towel.

"I'm awfully sorry," said the big black whale. "I didn't mean to get you wet."

"Oh, that's all right," said Peter with a gentle smile. "I've been wet before and I'm sure I'll get wet again." He walked toward the cabin of the boat as he said, "Well, I've been out long enough. I've got to get my catch in."

The fisherman gave a last wave and the old boat chugged away toward shore.

Serena glided over to the bubble. "Oh dear, I'm afraid I've totally lost my manners," she said to the travelers. "It is my extreme pleasure to introduce you to my cousin, the president of the Underwater Confederation, Seetasha the Right Whale."

Seetasha let out a low, rumbling chuckle and the children giggled.

"We've already met, but I officially welcome you to Earth, Professor," said the great whale. "And, as our guest, if there's anything I can do to assist you with your mission here, please don't hesitate to ask."

"Yes," sang out Serena, "there's nothing we wouldn't do for you."

"Well, actually, there is something you can do, President Seetasha. I need to find pure, clean water so I can get home to Quantia for the Rainbow Festival."

"Hmm," said the whale. Ripples and tiny waves washed over her back as she thought. "I remember a place from when I was very young—a place where pure, cold, fresh water always flows out from beneath the ocean floor. It's quite a ways from here but I'm sure I can find it again."

The professor's eyes sparkled like the sea and all four ears stood straight up as he heard the news. "When can we leave?" he asked.

"Why, now! Just follow me. Bye, Serena. Bye, Dazzle and Chakra," she called out. Then the fifty-five-foot, seventy-ton mammal flapped her gargantuan tail and dove gracefully into the water.

Angelicus and the children bid farewell to their friends, the dolphins.

Little Chakra swam in a circle around the bubble.

"Maybe someday we'll go swimming together, Zak," he whistled.

"For sure!" Zak yelled back.

Angelicus pushed on the pipe. "I think we'll do better if we stay above Seetasha," he said as the bubble rose into the air.

A group of shorebirds flew past. "Howdy, Professor. How's it going?"

"Just terrific, my friends," he responded.

The rays of the setting sun shined through the clouds and streaked across the sky. The wind blew from the north and the bubble headed south over the shimmering coral and lavender blue sea. The adventurers followed the great whale.

THE WATERSPOUT AND AN
EXPLOSION UNDER THE SEA

Small houses, ships, boats, and marinas dotted the coastline. Surging breakers spread an apron of foam across the shifting frontier between land and sea. The color of the ocean—indigo blue, dark green, and aqua—changed below them as the bubble headed farther and farther south.

The sun was rising and the wind blew across the surface of the water. Whitecaps glistened on the current like tiny tufts of mountain snow.

Angelicus looked down and said, "Do you see Seetasha, kids?"

The children peered out.

"No," said Zak, "but look at that big white ship. It must be a cruise ship."

Ziggy barked and wagged his tail excitedly.

"There's Seetasha," yelled Ivy. "She's coming up for air. But the ship is heading straight toward her. She's gonna get hit—Professor, do something!"

Angelicus shifted gears on the pipe and the bubble raced down toward the water.

"Look out, Seetasha! Watch out!" shouted Zak and Ivy.

The magnificent creature surfaced and, hearing the children's screams, swerved away from the huge ship, just missing it.

"Thanks, kids," she called out. "That was a close call. A lot of my brothers and sisters have died being run over by ships. That's one of the reasons there aren't too many of us left. You'd think they would have noticed us by now."

"Yeah," said Zak, "you're on the endangered species list."

"What?" said Seetasha, shocked. "List? You mean the humans are concerned about us?"

"Sure we are," answered Zak. "Lotsa people are trying to clean up the ocean and protect the whales."

"Well, that's a relief. Maybe there is hope. Heaven knows we need it. All the junk being dumped into the sea is poisoning our food."

She stopped for a minute and thought. "But come to think of it, I've heard a song echoing in the ocean currents. My cousins, the humpbacks, were singing it. Something about humans getting together to clean up an awful oil spill up north somewhere, and washing off the ducks and seals. I thought it was just a rumor, a folk song. I guess it's true. Of course, the whole Earth depends on the ocean for food. Even the humans."

"Oil spill?" said Angelicus. "Really! Who spilled oil into the water? Why would they do that?"

"One of those ships," Seetasha replied, "collided with an iceberg."

"Weren't the Guardian Residents watching? Don't they know you can't mix oil and water?" One of the professor's eyes turned gray and the other one bright red.

Ivy glanced nervously to Zak, who looked concerned, and Ziggy cringed, but the whale went on talking before Angelicus could launch into one of his tirades.

"But hopefully, where I'm taking you, the water's still flowing clean, Professor," she said. "Of course, I haven't been there in years."

"How much farther do you think we have, President Seetasha?" asked Zak.

"Oh," she replied, "we're almost there."

Seetasha dove back into the water and continued south, staying just below the surface. The bubble followed, surfing across the tops of the waves.

As they moved along, islands appeared. The air grew warm and tropical. Palm trees reached out over bright white beaches. A group of pelicans glided slowly past, staying low over the water, their wings barely moving.

"Hey, Ivy, look at those pelicans. They're in perfect formation—like a bomber squadron!" exclaimed Zak.

Ivy laughed. "And there are the shorebirds. I think they're the same ones from the bay."

Sure enough, a flock of red knots swooped down excitedly and called out. The children and Angelicus waved back and Ziggy barked "Hello."

Suddenly the sun disappeared and the sky grew dark. The wind howled.

Zak looked down through the bubble floor. "Professor," he yelled, "the ocean is rising!"

The bubble began spinning, bouncing like a rubber ball on the waves surging beneath them.

"What's going on?" cried Ivy, holding onto her rocking chair for dear life.

Ziggy whimpered and clutched his paws around Zak's neck.

"It's a waterspout!" exclaimed Angelicus. "First cousin to the tornado. Isn't it wonderful?" His eyes turned bright blue and his ears spun around and around like four pinwheels. "Hear the wind? Hear the water?"

Zak smiled and said, "This is phenomenal."

"It's no phenomenon, Zak. It's just like the bubble. The sun, the wind and the water have a powerful partnership. They're all working together. The ocean is the battery for your Big Blue Ball. You see, when the sun warms the water, the water heats the air and the air makes the wind. Then the wind blows on the water until the waves are moving faster than the wind itself! That's how the temperature transfers across your whole planet. That's what keeps you warm. A spectacular sharing of energy if I've ever seen one! Would you kids like to go to the top of this waterspout?"

"Can we, Professor?" asked Zak.

"Of course we can," he responded.

Ziggy wagged his tail and barked.

"Well then, hold onto your chairs and enjoy the ride."

Angelicus pushed the purple button on the pipe and the bubble balanced itself on top of the erupting waterspout as it rose into the air. It climbed higher and higher toward the clouds until they were miles in the air and they were spinning around and around the peak of the gigantic swaying column of water and swirling wind.

"This is extremely excellent, Professor!" hollered Zak. "It's better than an amusement park!"

"Zak, I'm getting dizzy," cried Ivy. "Like being on top of a dream!"

Seetasha was staring up at them from far below. Her voice called out faintly over the roar of the waterspout, "Professor, stop fooling around. Are you going to keep playing up there all day? You better get down here. It's time to go under the water."

Angelicus' eyes turned blush pink with embarrassment. "Sorry, Seetasha," he yelled, "we'll be right down." He turned to the children. "Watch this, kids. Hang on!"

He pulled back hard on the pipe, gave it a twist, and let go of the controls. The pipe let out a squawk, all the lights flared and the stem spun around. The bubble started rolling down the side of the waterspout. It rolled and rolled until the roll turned into a slide and down they all slid, faster and faster. They splashed onto the water and the bubble bounced three times, coming to rest alongside Seetasha.

"Are you done?" she asked dryly.

Sheepishly, Angelicus grinned. The children giggled.

"Oh, Seetasha," said Ivy, out of breath, "that was fun!"

"I'm glad you had fun," replied the cetacean crustily. "Once in a while you've got to let yourself go. You can't take life too seriously." She laughed and asked Angelicus, "Can you attach your bubble to my back, Professor?"

The professor nodded.

"Good," she said. "We might make better time."

Suddenly Zak remembered he had to be home in time for

dinner, and glanced at his watch. The hands were stopped. Angelicus was deeply engrossed with the pipe. He pushed the blue button. The stem lit up and, in an instant, a sharp breeze blew up from the west. It carried the bubble up onto the back of Seetasha's head and the craft landed directly behind her V-shaped blowholes, molding itself to her giant body.

"Docking mechanism activated," announced the pipe.

"Ready?" called out Seetasha.

"Ready," answered Angelicus.

The next thing they knew, the four passengers were riding the great whale as she descended gracefully into the ocean.

"Hey, Ivy," said Zak, "isn't it great down here?"

"Yeah," Ivy answered, "like a garden under the sea."

The sunlight sparkled down from the surface, lighting the brilliant underwater garden of multihued corals, sponges, anemones and seaweeds.

A magical striped parrotfish was swimming between a cluster of orange-colored tube sponges as the awed divers glided past. Ziggy pressed his little black nose against the bubble to see. He sniffed as a fantastic assortment of sea creatures—jellyfish and sand dollars, garibaldi fish and sea stars, and even an unlikely-looking zebra shark—gathered around the bubble.

They called out, "Welcome to Earth. Welcome to the Underwater Confederation, Professor."

"Why, thanks for having me," he answered wholeheartedly.

Like an immense, living, underwater vessel, Seetasha carried her passengers farther and farther into the depths of the ocean and the deeper they went, the dimmer the light grew.

"Professor, it's getting awfully dark down here," whispered Zak.

"No problem." Angelicus touched the yellow button on the pipe and the bubble began to glow, illuminating the water around them.

A manta ray glided past, its wings flapping slowly. A giant squid shimmered in the dark water beneath them, lighting the way for a blue crab, scuttling across the sandy ocean floor.

The children were so mesmerized by the underwater world that they barely noticed they had come to rest near the base of an immense undersea cliff. A cry from Seetasha shook the bubble and startled them awake. Angelicus' ears stood up straight. Ziggy jumped from Zak's lap and growled.

"Oh no!" wailed the whale. "Oh my goodness gracious!"

"What's wrong?" called out Angelicus.

"I'm afraid I have bad news for you," she answered. "Shine your light over there. Just past my nose."

Angelicus jiggled the stem of the pipe and a beam of light flooded the caves along the cliff. There they saw an awful sight: a huge stack of fifty-gallon drums, strewn topsy-turvy along the ocean floor. They were seeping a steaming black fluid into the water.

Ivy pointed out a warning label on one of the drums—a skull and crossbones above some lettering. "Professor, that's toxic!" she shrieked.

"Oh dear," he said, "why do the humans dump those chemicals into the sea? If they don't want them, why do they think the water would want them? What do they do with that slimy stuff, anyway?"

"I don't know what they do with it," cried Seetasha, "but it sure doesn't belong here. This is where the fresh underwater stream was. Oh, this is horrible!"

Angelicus asked, "Seetasha, are you sure?"

She lowered her eyes. "I'm afraid so," she answered.

"These are troubled waters, indeed," he sighed. "Troubled waters, indeed." He drooped his head.

Zak's heart grew heavy and a tear came to Ivy's eye. Ziggy whimpered and licked Angelicus' hand. Far worse things were happening on Earth than even Deer had told him.

Zak was beginning to wonder if his new friend was ever going to get home to Quantia. He thought, "If only I could do something."

"Maybe the water's still all right, Professor," offered Zak hopefully. "If we could just move those drums out of the way."

Angelicus brightened up. "That's a wonderful thought, Zak. But I'm afraid the damage has been done. That muck is in the water and the water isn't free to sparkle the way it once did." He put his hand on Zak's shoulder.

Ziggy growled and hunched down close to the floor.

The professor cocked his head and stretched his four green ears out toward the open sea. "By golly, you're right, Ziggy," he said.

"What is it?" asked Ivy.

"Listen carefully. . . . Hear it?" responded Angelicus. His ears twitched.

Zak exclaimed, "I hear it!"

A low rumble could be heard moving toward them across the ocean floor. The cliff began to sway and the alarmed fish darted off in all directions.

"What is it, Professor?" yelled Zak.

"It's just your Big Blue Ball stretching," answered Angelicus. "Shifting its crust. The rock is moving to get more comfortable."

"You mean an earthquake?" hollered Ivy.

"An earthquake?" chirped Seetasha. "We have to get away from this cliff!" She started swimming toward open water.

"Wait, Seetasha," called Angelicus, "we can't leave those drums. We're going to have to deal with this."

The drums had been knocked loose from their precarious perches and were bouncing around on the ocean floor.

"Are they gonna explode?" yelled Ivy.

"I'm not sure," Angelicus said, "but we can't take any chances. We've got to move fast. Seetasha, hold steady. I've got to blow a double bubble."

"A double bubble? How do you do that?" asked Zak.

"Not now, my boy. Just watch. There's no time to waste!"

He pushed on the green button, took a deep breath and blew with all his might into the pipe. A new bubble began to grow on the outside wall of the craft and expanded till it was just large enough for one occupant. Taking the pipe and tucking it under his arm, he stepped into the new bubble and began floating toward the now smoldering pile of drums.

"Be careful, Professor," called out Seetasha.

With a determined nod and a wink toward the children, Angelicus turned to the business at hand, guiding the little bubble close to the chemicals. Flames were coming from one of the canisters and a sizzle could be heard through the water.

The professor blew hard on the pipe and a third bubble grew off the second one. The new one sent out several long, finger-like appendages over the dumpsite. Like a giant hand, it reached out and gathered the gyrating, burning drums together. Spreading itself over the toxic pile, it sealed itself tightly to the ocean floor.

CHAPTER TWELVE

Zak exclaimed, "That's real bubble power!"

Angelicus raced back, merged his little bubble with the bubble craft and, with a pop, rejoined the children and Ziggy.

"Good job, Professor," said Seetasha.

"And just in time," Angelicus answered, puffing.

Sure enough, the ocean floor began to tremor and quake, rocking the containers in the bubble.

"Look, Professor," yelled Zak, "the lids are blowing off!"

BOOM! BANG! BAM!

The canisters were expanding and exploding like underwater bombs. Foamy black and green liquids, orange and red flames, and brown and yellow smoke swirled around creating an evil-looking stew inside the bubble.

"Eew! Yuck!" yelled Ivy, "What *is* that?"

The children watched, horrified, as a hideous demonic face appeared in the raging inferno. It was shifting and changing shape and blood-curdling screams came from its mouth. Horns grew out of the middle of its head.

His voice shaking, Zak yelled, "It looks like the devil!"

"It's that vile varmint, Borrell," said Angelicus. "Every evil thought and jealous, greedy, ugly feeling has come to the surface. They're written all over its face. See it? There's the whole thing in a nutshell. A complete waste of life energy!"

Ziggy cringed and Ivy and Zak clutched each other, shivering.

"Look," yelled Zak, "the monster's changed into a man!"

"Yeah," said Ivy, "it looks like a man I've seen on TV."

A smiling, friendly salesman had replaced the evil, scowling face of Borrell.

They heard a telephone ring through the water and the man

in the bubble reached down for it. "Hello," he answered pleasantly, then paused. "Professor," he called out, "it's for you."

"Ignore him," cautioned Angelicus.

"No, really," called the man again, "don't believe me. Listen!" He held the receiver out toward them and they heard a recorded computer voice. It sounded rather like the pipe.

"Hello. I have an important message for you," said the voice. "Congratulations, Professor Angelicus. You have won your choice of three grand prizes being held in *your* name! To claim your choice of an all-expense paid trip to anywhere on Earth for four, a Superior Bubble Pipe with new hyper-sparkle power unit, or a one-week's unlimited supply of absolutely *pure* water, simply call this toll-free number now. Dial 1-800-PURE-H20 from this telephone in the next five minutes and all your dreams will come true. This is a once in a lifetime opportunity, so *call now*!"

"Professor," said Zak, "listen! Pure water! You can go home to Quantia!"

Angelicus grabbed Zak by the shoulders. His eyes turned a clear sky blue. "Don't listen. It's Borrell. And he's lying. Don't you see? If I take that telephone, I'll have to open the bubble. There's no pure water waiting on the other end of that line. That's just another one of Borrell's evil, manipulating games. That monster has no soul and no conscience. It will do anything to put you under its spell. We could watch for an eternity and never see the end of that hooligan's awful show."

"Gosh, I really believed it," said Zak.

Ziggy sniffed. He knew all along it was Borrell!

"Seemed fishy to me," chimed in Seetasha.

"I didn't believe it for a minute," said Ivy. "I knew it was bogus. That was awful and cruel. To try and get your hopes up like that, Professor."

"That's very kind, Ivy, but I wasn't fooled. I've lived long enough to know that Borrell can turn any good dream into a nightmare—take hope and make it seem hopeless," said the professor sadly.

Borrell was getting madder and madder because Angelicus hadn't fallen for his tricks. The nice face distorted and twisted up viciously. He flew into a temper tantrum and mean, awful things, obscenities and insults exploded from his mouth. "Little girl," Borrell shrieked, "there are no magic bubbles! And don't you know? You'll never get home in time for dinner, little boy. And you—you green-eared Quantian. I'll skin you and that little dog alive and see you both roasting over my coals!"

Zak grabbed Ziggy and held him close. "You stay away from Ziggy!" he yelled.

"Don't lose faith, Zak," called Angelicus. "Borrell is just trying to push your fear buttons."

Suddenly a roar came from Seetasha. "How *dare* you," she yelled, a stream of bubbles blasting from her blowholes, "terrorize and insult Angelicus and the children like that. As president of the Underwater Confederation, I won't stand for it!"

"Who do you think you're talking to, Queen Blubber," Borrell screamed back. "I'll make whale oil out of you!"

Ivy couldn't help but speak her mind. "Jerk!" she yelled.

"Now, now, Ivy, stay calm. You're just feeding that tyrannical trickster more fuel," said Angelicus. "He's just trying to burst your bubble."

Explosions were ripping holes in the monster's face. Borrell was howling and thrashing around in the bubble. The bubble looked like a ball of fire and the ocean rocked from the terrible racket.

Angelicus raised his bushy green eyebrows. "That monstrous magician can really put on a spectacle, can't he?"

"But Professor, what if Borrell gets out?" asked Zak nervously.

"Right now he can't escape. As long as we think positive and stay centered," Angelicus answered calmly. "Remember, we all have the power inside us to fight Borrell. He has no defense against beautiful thoughts and beautiful dreams. But that bubble can't last forever. A single evil deed or the littlest bit of fear will feed Borrell's ego and break the bubble.

"For now we'll just leave that demon here to stew in his own juices. We've wasted enough time on this nasty nightmare. We've got to keep going. We have to find pure water."

Ziggy noticed the professor get a faraway look in his eyes. A look of uncertainty crossed his face and his flower antenna drooped a little. Ziggy knew what Angelicus was thinking. The professor was sad about Nega and missed his home, Quantia. The Sharelings were probably busy getting ready for the Rainbow Festival. The little dog jumped up into Angelicus' arms and licked his face.

"Oh, thank you, Ziggy," said the professor, perking up. "You're right, we've got to keep going. No time to be sad."

He set Ziggy down and called out, "Seetasha, where do you think we can go from here?"

"Well, Professor," she started, "we might—"

But her words were cut short by a gruff, authoritative voice that came from behind them. "I'll tell you where you're going," the voice said, "you're going to jail! You're all under arrest!"

CHAPTER TWELVE

Seetasha swung around in the water to confront the mysterious voice.

Like a nightmare looming in the darkness, a half-dozen sharks hovered, with the flickering flames of Borrell in the bubble reflected off their menacing, protruding teeth.

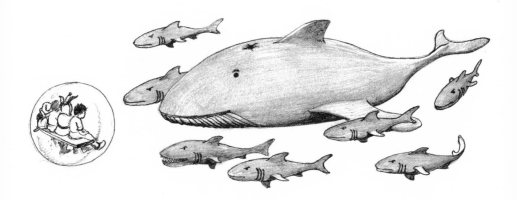

THE SHARK PATROL
AND POPADOPADON

"**A**rrest? Who, may I ask, are you, young shark? And just what are we under arrest *for*?" demanded Seetasha of the nearest of six goblin sharks blocking their way. Their jaws were exposed, baring their yellow, pointy teeth.

"We're the Shark Patrol. And you're all under arrest for disturbing the peace and for trespassing in sacred waters. Now, you better not make any waves, lady. Just come quietly and there won't be any trouble."

"Sacred! How sacred can these waters be if you've let humans contaminate them with toxic, explosive waste? Didn't you hear that explosion?" Her voice rumbled through the water.

A scallop opened its shell and its four blue eyes peeked out timidly from behind some ribbon grass.

"That's why we're here, lady. No explosions allowed, by orders of the palace. The Palace of Memories."

"Don't you know who I am?" she asked.

"No, ma'am, we don't," he answered through his bared teeth. He swaggered toward her. "Who *are* you?"

"Why, I'm President Seetasha," she answered, shocked.

"Sure, lady. And I'm Prime *Minister* Popadopadon!" He sneered and turned to his compatriots.

They all laughed and advanced menacingly.

"Well, I never! Where are your manners?" She called up to the bubble, "I'm sorry, Professor," she said, "there's just no respect anymore."

"What manners, lady? We're just working under palace orders. You'll have to come along with us."

"Well, you just call the prime minister right now and tell him you are about to arrest the president of the Underwater Confederation and Professor Angelicus of Quantia—who, I might add, just saved your life with the bubble he blew around that explosion."

Dubiously, the sharks conferred in silence. They turned back to the whale and her passengers, their weird horn-like snouts moving closer. The leader did not speak.

"Oh, never mind, I'll call him myself," she said impatiently.

She let out a long whistle so low it made the sharks' teeth rattle. After a few minutes she stopped and cocked her head to listen for a response.

"Professor," hissed Ivy, "who is Prime Minister Popadopadon?"

"I think my grandfather mentioned him in the *Planetary Guide*," answered Angelicus. "I think he's very old." He pulled out the tattered guidebook and rapidly thumbed through the pages. "Yes, here it is. Page twenty-nine. He's a reptile of some kind. Been here since before the Great Asteroid hit your Big Blue Ball."

"You mean . . . he's a *dinosaur?*" blurted out Zak.

"Wait, he's answering," said Angelicus. His ears perked up and he turned and whispered to the children, "Oh boy, are those sharks in trouble! I wouldn't want to be in their fins!"

Zak and Ivy giggled.

The goblin sharks swam back a few strokes and huddled their pinkish tan bodies together.

Seetasha called over to them. "Did you hear that, young shark?"

"Yes, ma'am," answered the lead shark, head down and tail up. There was no bite left in his bark. "We're awfully sorry, ma'am. If you'd be kind enough to follow us, we'll take you to the palace."

"Where are we going?" asked Ivy, excited.

"The Palace of Memories," answered Seetasha. "It holds all the records of the planet. It's very, very beautiful. I haven't been there since I was a calf, still in school."

Seetasha followed the sharks along the side of the cliff. Soon they came to a large opening just above the sea floor and the sharks separated, three to a side, and bowed gracefully.

"Excuse us, but before you enter, we'll have to ask you to turn down your lights. It will confuse the light creatures in the corridor."

"Ah, of course," said Angelicus, and turned down the pipe to a very dim glow.

The sharks waved them on and Seetasha, carrying the bubble on her back, glided through the opening into a long, high-ceilinged corridor.

At first the children couldn't see, but as their eyes adjusted, they saw that an unbelievable variety of glowing underwater creatures were lighting the way. There were funny-looking lantern fish with rows of lights running along their bodies, and fish with golden orbs dangling above their heads. One fish had transparent skin and bones that shone a brilliant green, and there was a scary-looking creature that was nothing more than a pair of giant, iridescent jaws.

Both sides of the corridor were lined with towering red and black striped columns. In the gloom the visitors could see the ruins of ancient walls, windows and hidden doorways.

"Professor," Ivy whispered, "how did this place get here?"

"Yeah," said Zak, "did fish build it? It looks like . . . like people built this."

"I'm not sure," Angelicus said softly. "I know it's been here a very long time. My grandfather said it was mentioned in an earlier guidebook."

The sharks led them on and on till they came to another grand corridor. The walls were gold and decorated from floor to ceiling with symbols: triangles, squares, hieroglyphs, and colorful drawings of the sun, the moon and the stars. In the far distance they could see a golden doorway.

In a hushed voice, Ivy said, "This looks like the pyramids in Egypt."

As they continued floating along the corridor, they passed room after room. Each one was filled to the brim with *things*!

The children were glued to their chairs in awe and Ziggy had his nose pressed against the wall of the bubble.

Ivy tugged at Zak's shirt. "Look, treasure chests and coins! And diamonds and emeralds!"

"Cool!" he responded. "And do you see that? Look at all the bones and skeletons! And look in that room! There's a pirate ship! And an airplane. And look—missiles and torpedoes, and . . . and in there . . . is that a flying saucer?"

"Gosh," Ivy said, "there's a Ferris wheel. What *is* this place?"

"It must be some sort of museum," Zak guessed. "There's everything under the sun here!"

"And above the sun, it would seem," responded Angelicus. "This place certainly tickles the imagination, doesn't it?" He laughed.

"The Palace of Memories is more like a school, Zak," called Seetasha. "We come here to learn how things have been before."

"How did you get everything here?" asked Zak. "I didn't know fish could do all this."

"Well, you'd be surprised what you can do with a little hard work and a little imagination," the whale said with a smile.

"As you know," she continued, "things have been falling into the sea for millions of years. Sharks and whales have swallowed them up, and octopuses, catfish, monkfish, angelfish, squirrelfish . . . all of the citizens of the sea have done their part: gathering these things up and bringing them here so we can keep a record of what has been going on . . . up on land as well as in the sea. Of course, a lot came from the humans. And we do wish they'd come pick some of it up. We can learn something from everything we see, but what do we do with it after that? It really doesn't belong down here and the water's not happy about it."

Angelicus solemnly rubbed his grassy green beard. "You

certainly have your work cut out for you, keeping the water clean. But you are doing the best with a bad situation."

They passed another room filled with thousands of bottles. They were arranged on racks by shape, size and color ... brown, green, blue, purple, yellow and white.

"President Seetasha," Ivy asked, "what is this room?"

"Well, I guess you'd call it a mail room," the whale answered. "It seems that humans communicate this way across the seas. There are messages in each one of these glass bottles. We've been trying to figure out how we can deliver them. 'Cause some of them have been here an awfully long time!"

Finally the sharks and the whale carrying the bubble arrived at the spectacular golden arched doorway. A hundred trumpet fish blared, drum fish drummed and a loud voice proclaimed: "Seetasha, President of the Underwater Confederation and her guests, Professor Aquius Botanicus Angelicus of Quantia, and Ivy, Zak, and Ziggy of the Land Dwellers!"

They entered the brilliantly lit room. It was filled with every sea creature imaginable and they were all honking and whistling and cheering, greeting the visitors. Giant oysters with giant pearls, glowing blue lobsters, and shining twenty-foot eels all welcomed the travelers as they floated up the center of the hall.

The walls of the palace's Great Hall were made of salt, sand, shells, and living coral of every color.

"Zak! This is like being inside a sandcastle!" said Ivy.

Zak nodded. "Yeah. Did you see the pictures?"

Painted on the sandy walls were people of all races and colors and of all time; all the animals of water, land and air; all the flowers and trees. All the history of the Earth was there.

Before they had a chance to take in any more of the sights, the walls shook with a roar like the children had never heard.

"Seetasha, my dear," the deep old voice rumbled, "it's so good to see you!"

With her passengers holding on for dear life, Seetasha raced happily through the long line of attendant fishes to the end of the long hall.

"Pop!" she blurted, then corrected herself. "Oh, dear me, I've forgotten my manners! Prime Minister, it *is* so good to see you!"

They had come to a table that was fifty feet high and ten times as long, and there the children saw the owner of the incredible voice. He was so gigantic, he looked like part of the room.

The giant voice chuckled. "You can still call me Pop, young lady. At my age, a reminder of youth is always refreshing. It's been so many years! Just look how you've grown up. Your parents must be very proud."

"Ivy," Zak whispered, "he *is* a dinosaur!"

"Yeah, but what kind? He looks like a dragon. He's bigger than anything—and look at his colors!"

Prime Minister Popadopadon was like nothing they had ever seen before. Even in science class, when they had studied dinosaurs, there wasn't anything like this gargantuan creature in their schoolbooks! His body was huge and it was colored like a marble . . . a swirling mix of every shade of green and blue, and his great armor-plated belly was white with red and orange polka dots. They couldn't even see the end of his tail and his head reached nearly to the ceiling of the colossal hall. As he looked down, the children counted three eyes, each one a different color. The left eye was orange and the right one was deep red. The third, right in the middle of his forehead, was a blazing bright yellow—like the color of the sun on a hot summer afternoon.

Zak asked, "Professor, why does he have three eyes?"

"Well, I understand each one sees something different," answered Angelicus. "The red eye sees the past, the orange one, the present, and the third eye—the yellow one—sees the future."

Ivy's own eyes were wide with wonder.

Seetasha spoke to the ancient sea creature again. "Pop, I'd like you to meet my friends, Professor Angelicus, Ivy, Zak, and Ziggy."

"Welcome, friends," came the huge voice again. "I'm so sorry about my guards. The problem is they don't seem to live long enough to remember one visitor from the next."

"Professor," continued Popadopadon, "it is good to have you back in these waters." He paused and slowly brought his extraordinary head close. The orange eye blinked. "But wait," he said. "You've changed. You've gotten younger somehow. No, that's not it. You're not the same, are you? You're not the same Professor Angelicus at all. Odd, but you do look like him."

"That's my grandfather you remember, Your Excellency," replied Angelicus good-naturedly. "He talked about you."

"Hmm." The dinosaur's eyes blinked one at a time, like strobe lights. "I hear you've had a close call. A quake. And Borrell as well. No broken fins, tails or hearts, I hope."

"No, we're fine, thank you, Your Excellency," said Seetasha. "Thank the tides Professor Angelicus had his bubble and tidied things up. It was awful! But Borrell is contained for now."

"I only wish we could have done more," added Angelicus.

"We never really contain Borrell, do we, Professor? He's always popping up," said Popadopadon, "so we just do our best. I must say Borrell and other leaders of darkness have taken an awfully strong position here on Earth in the last few centuries. They've gained followers—gotten them on their wavelength, so to speak. You must have seen Room 66 on your way in—all the missiles and guns—the instruments of hatred and war. It seems like some humans have forgotten how to follow their heart."

"I've noticed that, Prime Minister," agreed Angelicus. "Things have gotten out of alignment here. Hate makes more hate. Only love can make love. If the Guardian Residents balanced their body, mind and spirit, the Big Blue Ball would be better balanced."

"Of course, there have been many great leaders of kindness," added Popadopadon.

With a swoop of his long, scaly neck he pointed his snout toward the wall. Ivy noticed a picture of a nurse tending the sick.

"Here in the Palace of Memories, we try to keep up with things," he said, "hoping that knowing the past will help creatures avoid their ancestors' mistakes, but . . ." His voice faded off.

The travelers waited as he gathered his thoughts.

Then he took up again. "Anyway, the Earth always has the final word. It quakes, erupts and floods, and usually figures out a way to clean things up. Like that asteroid in my time!" He laughed. "That sure cleaned up a lot! Many good spirits rose up and left back then. Some went to other planets and some even went directly to the Great Universal Source. I hear from them from time to time."

Popadopadon noticed that the children were awestruck. He laughed. "Ha-ha, little air breathers, I don't suppose you've seen anything like me for some time—up there on land!"

The children couldn't answer.

"Well?" he went on. "Have you?"

"Well . . . well . . . no sir," Zak finally blurted out.

The sea dragon laughed again. "No, I suppose you haven't," he said, "and you're not likely to again. I'm afraid our days have passed. There are very few of us left. I have a couple of cousins trapped in inland seas here and there."

Zak interrupted. "Do you mean like the Loch Ness Monster? Is he your cousin?"

"She is my cousin," corrected Popadopadon. "And I might add, quite a lot younger than myself. But who in their right mind would want to live for seventy million years, anyway?"

"Uh, sir?" asked Ivy, hesitantly.

"Yes?"

"What kind . . . I mean . . . what species of dinosaur are you?" she responded bravely.

"I'm sorry, you'll have to speak up," said Popadopadon. "There seems to be something in my ear."

He shook his head, sending shock waves through the room and a red octopus raced out of the giant dinosaur's ear, trailing a cloud of purple ink.

"Ah, that's better," he roared. "Now. What was that?"

Ivy meekly repeated the question. "What kind of dinosaur are you?"

"Hmm. Good question," he answered. "I've always just been called the Popadopadon." His eyes flashed playfully and he added, "But you can call me Pop!"

He laughed again, then asked Professor Angelicus, "How is your grandfather, anyway? Does he still play that silly board game with the little squares? I never could get the best of him in that game."

"You must mean the game of Chips," answered Angelicus, smiling sadly. "He doesn't play anymore, I'm afraid. He's passed on. But he did love that game. He taught me to play when I was very young. I never could win from him, though. Even when I got older."

"Ah, I'm sorry to hear that," rumbled the prime minister. "He was a gentle soul. But maybe I have a chance to win with you. Perhaps we'll play a little later?"

"Well, Your Excellency, I'd like nothing better than to stop and visit for a few hundred years," answered Angelicus, "but I've got to get home to Quantia for the Rainbow Festival. I stopped here for some water to fuel my pipe, but I haven't been able to find any that's pure enough—that's sparkling clean. I was hoping maybe you could help. Things have really changed here since my grandfather's day."

"That they have, my boy. That they have," said Popadopadon. His long neck swayed sadly from side to side. "I haven't been to the surface for many years. I've got my little air supply here at the top of the palace and I've grown so large I don't think I could get out if I tried. But I don't hear good things from above. Not good things at all. Of course I've always seen it was going to happen—what with my third eye—the yellow one that sees the future. But a third eye will never stop you from feeling the sadness when you see terrible things."

He closed his red and orange eyes and the brilliant yellow one in the middle of his forehead flared. He grew silent and his head bobbed up and down. After a few minutes he blinked several times, coughed, and continued talking as if he had never stopped.

"But I have a dream," he said. "Well, maybe more than a dream. I see a sunny future for this planet. The humans have it in them, you know, to turn it all around—to set this planet back on its original course. I see it all happening. But they have to remember how to follow their hearts. Because only when you follow your heart and trust in your soul, only then does the mind start to work in the right way."

He seemed to doze off again for a second but abruptly woke back up. "But, water!" he boomed. "Water! We've got to get you some water!"

"Do you think you can help?" asked the professor.

"Well, let me see," answered Popadopadon. He stared straight ahead with his orange eye, closing the other two. "There are two possibilities," he said. "The first one's easier and second one is not. So I'd try the first one first, if you know what I mean. Before the second one, that is."

The children giggled, but quieted down when Angelicus looked around at them sternly.

"Which is the first choice?" asked Angelicus.

"Ah. The first choice," said the great reptile. His orange and yellow eyes closed. The red one stared off into space. "It's where I was hatched," he said. "At the beginning of the mighty Queen of Rivers . . . at the Waterfall of the Angels. There's lots of sparkle there, Professor. It's been sparkling since the beginning of time. And I don't think much has changed—except who lives there, of course. The insects are pretty much the same but, aside from them, it's mostly just mammals and birds. Seetasha and my sharks will know how to get you there."

He stopped and drifted for a minute before he went on. "There are a few of my distant relatives left but they're so little these days . . . alligators and such. Lizards."

He let out a giant sigh, causing the skin of the bubble to flutter like a flag on a windy day. "Ah, well," he yawned, "such is the way of life."

"Excuse me, Your Excellency," Angelicus said quietly, "the second?"

"The second what?" asked the fantastic lizard.

"The second choice. To find the water," the professor reminded him.

"Ah! Yes," said Popadopadon slowly, "that's more difficult. That's much more difficult. But of course you have that gadget—that bubble pipe. So maybe it won't cause you any problem. You'll be all right." The lids on his eyes drooped.

They all waited, but it seemed like he was falling asleep.

Finally Seetasha spoke up. "Pop? If you wouldn't mind, could you tell us where?"

Popadopadon abruptly opened his three eyes. "Ah, of course! Where. Thought I already told you, you know. Hard to remember what I've said and what I haven't."

He cleared his throat and continued. "Harrumph. Yes. On the cold continent—the Land of Light. Some call it the Land of Darkness, but they went there at the wrong time. It's at the bottom of the Earth."

He paused. "It wasn't always the bottom, you know. The Earth turned around once. Or was it twice? I'm not sure. That was long before my time. But there's water there . . . frozen long before I was hatched . . . bound to be pure. You'll have to look

CHAPTER THIRTEEN

for it, mind you. But it's there."

He nodded his head slowly. "It's there," he repeated, "but be careful. Be awfully careful. It's very cold." Then he drifted off to sleep.

Soon he was snoring soundly, and Seetasha said, "I think we'll just let him sleep." She swam up to the tip of his nose and puckering her big lips, gave him a kiss. "Goodbye, old dear," she said softly.

Seetasha turned and called to the leader of the Shark Patrol. "If you'd be so kind as to lead us back to the Southern Current, I can take our friends from there," she said to him.

"Yes, ma'am," answered the shark. He flicked his tail and signaled to the rest of the patrol, who were floating stiffly at the table.

"If you'll follow us, please," he said.

Gracefully the patrol led them out of the now quiet chamber. The travelers passed swiftly through the corridors, out of the palace and back into the open sea.

"Thank you, my friends," called Seetasha to the sharks. "I can find my way from here."

"Sorry for the inconvenience, ma'am," called the lead shark as the patrol disappeared into the darkness.

With the bubble on her back, Seetasha turned south and headed toward the mouth of the mighty Queen of Rivers.

THE RAIN FOREST

"**W**ell, Professor, here we are. I'm sorry, but I won't be able to take you up the river," said Seetasha.

"Well, Seetasha," answered Angelicus, "you certainly have done more than your share already."

"Oh, go on with you, now," she said. "It was nothing and it was my pleasure. I only wish I could have done more. You know, every morning I wake up and ask myself, 'Seetasha, what good deed can you do today?' And I can always find something. It always makes me feel good inside when I can be of help."

"Thank you, President Seetasha," said Angelicus. "You truly are a great leader of kindness and we will miss you. But it's time for us to get going."

"Well, if you need me for anything," said the whale, "just

call me through the ocean currents. I'll hear you."

Seetasha swam toward the surface as the professor fiddled with the controls. He pushed on the purple button twice.

"Air lock deactivating," said the pipe.

"Seetasha," Angelicus called out, "do you think you can give us a boost?"

"You mean with my blowholes?"

"Yes."

"No problem. Let me get us out of the water."

The great whale gained speed as Angelicus maneuvered the bubble directly over her blowholes.

"Hold on, kids," he said.

"Prepare for blastoff," called out the pipe.

Seetasha broke through the waves and, with a loud roar, released a huge blast of air from her blowholes. The bubble careered high into the air on her misty V-shaped plume.

"Goodbye, President Seetasha. Goodbye," the children and Angelicus called. Ziggy stood up on his hind legs, leaned against the skin of the bubble, and barked.

With a great kick of her tail, Seetasha rolled over and disappeared into the sea.

The sky was blue and clear. The sun blazed and the wind blew from the east, pushing the bubble toward the land. They flew up a large bay till it narrowed to a wide, majestic river. The treetops along its banks clustered together like giant green umbrellas and the deep forest stretched out below them. Indians in a canoe paddled their way through the current. A school of pink dolphins jumped up from the water.

Ziggy barked "Hello" and the children waved.

"How far do we have to go, Professor?" asked Zak.

"I'm not sure," answered Angelicus. "The bubble is on course and we'll just ride the wind till we see the great Water-falls of the Angels."

The bubble traveled up the river many, many miles. They could see smaller rivers and tributaries branching out into the vast, lush rain forest.

A brilliant flock of blue and red macaws rose up from muddy brown cliffs and flew past them.

Suddenly a huge cloud of black and yellow smoke appeared in the blue sky up ahead.

"Great balls of fire!" exploded Angelicus, his eyes flaring red. "What is going on here? What kind of monkey business is this? Is this the smoke we saw from outer space? Is this the burning of the tree Sharelings?"

They could see a fire raging and smell the burning of brush. Soot and ash fell in the air around them and the skin of the bubble began to turn gray.

"This is far worse than I could have ever imagined! We're going to have to land," cried out Angelicus.

"But, Professor," protested Zak, "are you sure? It doesn't look too safe down there. Look at those animals running toward the river!"

Flocks of birds were screaming and flying across the river to safety. Brown and white striped agoutis were racing along the water's edge and spider monkeys were leaping from tree to tree, trying to escape the advancing inferno.

"That's all the more reason to land, Zak," responded Angelicus. "There must be something we can do to help. Anyway, the ash and soot have weakened the bubble. We don't have enough power to get above the fire now."

The professor shifted gears and the bubble rapidly descended toward the riverbank. "We're going to have to make this quick," he said. "I can't save the water in the pipe, so prepare to hit the ground, kids." He pushed the red button on the pipe.

"Emergency evacuation," it called out.

With a pop, they were all rolling on the ground.

The air was thick with smoke and falling debris. Zak was up first and helped the others to their feet. Ziggy shook himself and went down to the river for a drink.

"Professor," panted Ivy, brushing herself off, "what are we gonna do?"

The children turned to Angelicus. His eyes had turned dark gray and his green ears were drooping down over his face.

"Oh dear," he said, "oh, my leaping lizards!"

In slow motion he scanned the clearing by the river's edge. He felt so sad. Banana, fig and rubber trees, beetles, butterflies, hummingbirds, snakes, iguanas, orchids, and passion flowers . . . an abundance of life. He could hear the cries of the creatures of the beautiful rain forest ringing in his ears.

"Oh, all these wonderful trees," he said, "each tree a home to so many thousands of Sharelings . . . and all their lives being threatened by this fire."

Flames were raging out of control in the forest beyond, coming closer by the minute. Angelicus' nostrils flared and he gasped for breath in the heated, smoky air.

Nearby, at the upper edge of the clearing, Zak noticed a peculiar green plant. It looked just like a gigantic Venus flytrap, and had two long, thick stalks. At the top of each stalk was a big green flower with red spiked leaves. Flames flared and flickered from its petals and the air was filled with the sweet smell of its nectar.

Zak started walking toward the plant.

Angelicus called out, "Zak, be careful!"

But Zak didn't hear the warning. He was overwhelmed by the sweet perfume and was drawn like a bee to honey toward the exotic plant. As the boy got closer, he saw drops of shimmering golden nectar oozing from the hairy, purple tooth-like spikes. He felt dizzy from its powerful scent and his vision began to blur. Suddenly the flower jumped forward, snapping at Zak with its huge jaw-like leaves.

"Watch out," screamed Ivy, "it's a snap trap, Zak!"

Ziggy barked ferociously.

Zak tried to jump but he was stuck! His feet were sinking into the mud.

"Quicksand!" he thought in horror. In a stupor, he struggled to break free, but the harder he tried the more stuck in the muck he became. The venomous plant loomed over him, its glistening poisonous spikes as large as daggers. Zak tried to shrink from its advance but the plant grabbed hold of his arm and started to pull him down under the ground.

"Help, Ivy, help!" he screamed. Zak's body was buried up to his neck in mud. "It's no use," he thought. "This is the end."

Angelicus called out to him: "Zak, stay calm. Don't panic. That plant has no roots. It's a bad dream—it's Borrell the Imposter!"

"The professor's right," Zak thought to himself. "This is a nightmare. I have to think positive. I've got to turn this bad dream around."

Ivy and Ziggy raced across the clearing.

Lying down on her stomach, Ivy reached out and yelled, "Give me your hand, Zak. Give me your hand!"

Ziggy snarled and fearlessly attacked the plant, trying to save his best friend.

Zak stretched his hand to Ivy and she grabbed hold of it. With all her might she pulled and pulled till finally, with a "slurp," he broke free and they scrambled onto firmer ground. The shaken children rose to their feet and held each other close. Ziggy jumped into Zak's arms and licked his face.

The children faced the man-eating plant and, in the center of its carnivorous leaves, they could see Borrell's monstrous face.

"Concentrate," said Ivy.

Zak and Ivy held hands and tightly closed their eyes. Ivy let her thoughts return to the pretty flowers in her mother's garden. Ziggy started dreaming of a big bone he had buried in the backyard.

But Zak couldn't concentrate. He couldn't help but wonder to himself what would make a plant grow like this. What kind of a seed did this plant come from?

Angelicus heard his thoughts and Zak heard the professor's gentle answer in his heart.

"It's not the seed, Zak. That plant grew in a pocket of negative energy. Treat any seed badly and you'll get a bad seed. And that gives Borrell a place to grow. Seeds need tender loving care and nurturing. Without the proper environment . . . a safe soil to grow up in and the food of unconditional love, it will grow all twisted and confused. It's the same for all Sharelings in all the worlds."

Finally Zak knew what he had to do. He had the power inside him to get rid of Borrell once and for all. No more nightmares. He wasn't afraid. He closed his eyes and pictured his coolest, most excellent dreams coming true.

Ivy looked at the ferocious plant. It was shrinking and its hairy spikes were spitting angry balls of fire.

The children heard a voice, raspy and ugly. "I'll be back," it said, "I'll be back. You can't always have good thoughts!"

"How much do you want to bet?" yelled Zak.

The plant got smaller and smaller, shrinking down into an ugly little gray seed. A green shoot tried to grow up from the mud, but it shriveled away and died. Then the dried, crinkly shell of the seed broke open and they could see there was nothing left inside. Slowly, the pieces sank into the quicksand and disappeared.

"Boy!" said Zak, and shuddered.

"Yeah," said Ivy.

The children turned and raced back to the professor.

"Are you OK, Zak?" asked Angelicus.

"I'm OK," answered Zak, "and I don't think Borrell's gonna bother us again!"

"Professor," cried Ivy, "the fire's getting worse. We have to do something!"

The flames had moved closer to the edge of the clearing.

"Yes," the professor said slowly, "something. We must do something. We must put this fire out—stop this infernal destruction. It's taking so many valuable lives. I'm shocked your Guardian Residents don't try to prevent these fires!"

"Umm . . . Professor," said Zak, "I'm afraid this fire might have been started by the Guardian Residents. To clear the land."

"Oh no," said Angelicus, and sadly he hung his head.

Zak added quickly, "But there are some people trying to stop them."

Angelicus raised his head and looked at the children. He

seemed dazed and disoriented. His eyes were so filled with gray tears he could barely see.

Ivy asked, "Professor, what's wrong? You're not yourself."

"No, I guess I'm not," gasped the professor. "This smoke doesn't agree with me at all. But there's no time for me. Do you see any frogs? We need the frogs."

Confused, Zak looked around until he spotted one. "Over there, Professor, on those lily pads."

"Good," said Angelicus. "This smoke is burning my eyes. I'm afraid I can't see him. You'll have to lead me."

The nervous children each took one of his hands and led him down to the riverbank.

"Here, Professor," said Zak, "right in front of you."

"Ah, yes," he said. "Young frog? I'm afraid I can't see you very well. Can you hear me? Do you know who I am?"

The bright green frog looked up at them with large, cat-like yellow eyes. "Of course I do, Professor. You're Angelicus of Quantia," it said with a croak. "My name is Daido."

"How do you do, Daido," said the professor. "I need your help."

"My help? With what—the fire? How can *I* help?"

"Usually I can call on a planet's powers," said the professor, "but I'm feeling very weak. The burning of all these hydrocarbons in the air is taking my breath away . . . and the heat . . . we Quantians can't handle this toxicity. This massacre is sapping my life force. I know you usually sing at night, but we need rain and we need it now."

"I know," said Daido.

The children stared quizzically.

"Professor," asked Zak, "what are you talking about?"

"The song of the frogs can bring on the rain," he answered. "They sing to the thunder spirits. Daido knows what I'm talking about."

"He's right, children," said the frog. "That's one of our jobs here on Earth. I could try to sing, even though it's daytime. And maybe all the other frogs will join me. But I can't guarantee anything. There aren't as many of us as there used to be. I don't know why, but our eggs have stopped hatching. So we'll have to sing twice as loud, but we can try our best."

"I saw a show on TV," said Ivy, "on the Discovery Channel. They said frogs are disappearing everywhere on the Earth."

Ziggy barked. He'd noticed it, too. He'd wondered why there weren't as many toads. He loved playing with them.

"Ultraviolet," said Zak.

"What?" asked Angelicus.

"Ultraviolet light," Zak repeated, "from the ozone hole. There's a hole in the ozone layer around the Earth."

Angelicus shook his head sadly in response to the terrible news. His wilted green ears flopped from side to side.

Daido swayed back and forth on the lily pad a few times and looked up at the sky. He swelled up his throat and let out a long whistle like the sound of the wind blowing through the trees. A gentle breeze came from the north, clearing the air of smoke. The frog stopped, cocked his head and whistled again. Almost immediately the air around them came alive. The sounds of croaks, clicks, chirps, barks, and taps answered Daido's call. Glorious choirs of frogs were all singing their hearts out.

Angelicus' ears perked up for a minute and a faint smile came to his lips. "What beautiful music to my ears," he whispered weakly. "What a beautiful song you sing, Daido."

Within minutes a group of black clouds blew up the river from the southeast, a huge clap of thunder roared across the sky, and the trees in the forest shook. A torrential rain came pouring down over the fire.

"Thank you, Daido," Angelicus said. "You truly are a great group of musical Sharelings if I've ever heard one. Now, thanks to you, the rain and the thunder spirits, some lives will be spared."

"It was our pleasure, Professor. I'm glad we could be of help. I hope you're feeling better." The bright green frog hopped into the water.

"Professor," said Zak, "we should get out of this rain."

"There," said Ivy, "under that tree. We can stay dry under there."

Raindrops were rolling off the tips of the thick, waxy leaves of a rubber tree that reached out over the river.

"I'm so tired," said Angelicus. He coughed. "I feel dizzy and lightheaded." He coughed again and his knees buckled.

The children rushed to hold him up.

"We'll help you, Professor," said Zak.

The children each held one of his arms and gently guided him to the haven of the great old tree. He collapsed against its trunk.

The air was filled with thick, steamy smoke and reeked with the smell of wet ashes. Dimly, they could see the skeletons of scorched trees, bushes and vines, still smoldering.

Angelicus wriggled his nose and sniffed. He could barely breathe. "Oh," he moaned, "where is the sweet smell of the flowers and the fresh earth? This air . . . has been stripped of . . . life."

"Zak," hissed Ivy, "he's really sick. We can't stay here. What're we gonna do?"

Zak thought for a moment, then exclaimed, "Quick, Professor—your pipe! Let me put some water in your pipe and we'll get out of here!"

Zak took the bubble pipe from Angelicus' belt. He reached out and let some of the raindrops that were dripping off the leaves of the rubber tree run into the bowl. When it was filled he placed it between Angelicus' teeth. Weakly, the professor reached up and grasped the pipe. He blew and blew, but to no avail. No bubble appeared.

Sadly, he looked at the children. "It's . . . no . . . use," he said. "It's . . . no use."

The children had to lean close to hear him.

"I'm afraid it . . . may . . . be . . . too late," he gasped. "I can't . . . even . . . blow . . . a bubble. I'll never get home to Quantia . . . and the Rainbow Festival. Oh, you poor children, look what I've gotten you into! And you're such true Sharelings."

"Professor, you're gonna be all right!" exclaimed Zak desperately. "Don't lose faith, not now! You told us yourself never to lose faith! Look, the rain is almost over. The fire's almost out and I *know* we're close to the pure water. Popadopadon *told* us."

Angelicus' green ears had turned brown and brittle at the edges. His flower antenna wilted over his forehead. A brownish yellow petal fell off and drifted to the ground. A big gray tear rolled down his cheek.

Ivy knelt down beside him and reached over to stroke his forehead. "Zak," she said, "we have to do something. I can feel his heart inside my own heart. And it's breaking."

Ziggy had been standing by, his ears down and his tail

tucked between his legs, sadly watching his friend weakening. He knew what he had to do. He walked over and, with a whimper, licked away the big gray tear from the professor's face. Then he slowly backed away and started quietly inching toward the forest's edge. As he slipped into the thicket, Zak realized he was leaving.

Zak called out, "Ziggy, come back! You'll get burned!"

Zak jumped to his feet and chased after him but Ziggy was nowhere in sight. The little dog had disappeared into the dense undergrowth.

"Oh no," Zak cried in desperation, "now Ziggy's gone!"

He ran back to Angelicus. The professor was lying deathly still and Ivy was kneeling beside him.

She put her head to his chest. "Professor, Professor!" she cried, and looked up at Zak. "I don't think he's breathing, Zak. Our environment is killing him. I think he's dying. Oh, Professor!" With tears streaming down her face, she cradled Angelicus' head in her arms.

"Are you sure he's not breathing?" Zak asked somberly. He knelt down and held his cheek close to the stricken alien's nose. "You're right," Zak said, "I can't feel any breath. Quick, Ivy, let's try mouth-to-mouth resuscitation. Like they taught us in lifeguard class. You push on his chest and I'll try breathing for him."

Holding the professor's nose shut, Zak blew hard into his mouth.

"Now, push, Ivy, push!" he panted.

Ivy pushed down with all her might on their friend's chest. Again and again they tried, but there was no response.

"It's not working," said Zak. "We're losing him!"

"Oh, Zak," wailed Ivy, "what are we gonna do? Ziggy's gone, and the professor's dying!"

"I'm gonna go get some help. There's got to be people around here somewhere."

"But Zak," she said, "I'm scared. Be careful. And don't get lost!"

"Don't worry, Ivy," said Zak, gently taking her hand, "I'll be back."

He pointed up at the blue sky. "See?" he said. "Things are clearing up. The fire's out and there's the sun. We're gonna be OK. You stay here and take care of the professor and I'll be back as fast as I can."

The boy looked around the clearing, trying to figure out the best route to take when Ziggy burst through the underbrush. His fur coat was covered with brambles and mud. He was panting hard and his little pink tongue was hanging out of the side of his mouth.

Ivy yelled, "Look, Zak! Ziggy's back!"

Right behind the little dog were hundreds of jungle animals, walking on the ground, swinging in the trees, and flying through the air. There were capybaras, kinkajous, squirrels and monkeys; black bears, anteaters, snakes, lizards and turtles. There were thousands of butterflies and birds of every shape and variety. They were scarlet, purple, yellow, indigo and orange . . . every color imaginable. A harpy eagle landed high on a kapok tree. A pair of giant condors soared in the sky. Orchid bees, beetles and dragonflies buzzed overhead. Sluggishly tagging behind was a giant, three-toed sloth. Every animal of the rain forest was there and a sleek, pure black jaguar was leading them all.

Zak looked at all the animals and then back at Ziggy. "Way to go, Ziggy! Good boy!"

Ziggy barked, jumped up and kissed him on the face.

The black jaguar spoke up. "I'm Reiki," he said, "Medicine Chief. And these are my rain forest friends. Ziggy came and told us Professor Angelicus is sick. We've come to heal him."

"But . . . but how?" Zak asked, puzzled.

The jungle animals all started talking at once. "How? With love, of course! He needs love! Love, love, love," they chanted.

"Love can mend his broken heart," purred Reiki, "and raise his spirits. It can give him the strength to heal."

The birds began a beautiful song; the animals gathered around the professor, kissing and licking him; and Ziggy joined in. The children smiled.

"Zak," whispered Ivy as she cradled Angelicus' head in her arms, "it looks like he's beginning to breathe!"

The professor's ears twitched and he weakly opened his eyes. They were pale blue. "Oh, look at all these good-hearted Sharelings," he mumbled. He blinked and closed his eyes once more.

"Zak," cried Ivy, "is he slipping away again?"

Before Zak could answer, they heard a gruff voice call from the edge of the forest. "I wondered where all these animals were going," it said.

Surprised, the children turned and saw a bearded man in a tattered safari hat limping out of the jungle with a walking stick made from a branch. His hiking boots and droopy white socks were streaked with mud and he was wearing a raggedy shirt and khaki shorts. His glasses hung cockeyed across his face and he carried a knapsack on his back.

"Fascinating," he said as he limped closer. "I wouldn't expect to see this many creatures in a lifetime of exploration. Let alone all together."

Ivy asked, "Who are you?"

"Why, I'm Doctor Good . . . Good without an 'e'," replied the grungy-looking character. "Doctor Dewing S. Good. At your service, young lady. And what have we here?"

"Doctor?" exclaimed Zak. "Boy! We need a doctor!"

"How so?" asked Doctor Good.

"Our friend, the professor," answered Ivy, "he's very sick—from the fire. The animals came to heal him with love. He's doing better but he's still unconscious. We don't know what to do."

"Terrible thing, these fires," said the doctor. "There are thousands, maybe millions of unknown species here and these fires are killing them before we even get a chance to study them. But I'm afraid I'm not a medical doctor, young lady. I'm a biologist and botanist, here in the rain forest doing research on plants and animals."

"But he's part plant *and* part animal," said Zak, excited.

"Really!" exclaimed Good. "Well, let's have a look, then."

He pushed his way through the animals and leaned over the professor. He glanced at Angelicus, then back at the children.

"Hmm," he said, "not from around here, is he? I've never seen a specimen like this. Interesting."

"No, he isn't," said Zak, "and he isn't a specimen. This is Professor Angelicus from Quantia. He's come to our planet for pure water so he can get back home."

"Yeah," added Ivy, "for the Rainbow Festival."

"Well, who or whatever he is, it looks like he's down for the count. Not in very good shape." The doctor didn't look hopeful.

He reached over and lifted one of Angelicus' brittle ears and peered inside. Then he pulled open a big eyelid, examined the eyeball closely, and let it shut. He picked up the professor's antenna. It gave a feeble twitch, then the flower broke off and crumbled to the ground. Finally Good took his knapsack off his back, fumbled through it, and pulled out a stethoscope. He put it to Angelicus' chest and listened.

"Well," he said, "his heart sounds good. It's pumping away, but that's about all I can say. He seems to be a highly sensitive creature from a very balanced planet. But he's completely out of whack. His whole immune system has gone haywire. He's out of balance. He's toxic, totally toxic."

"Is he gonna be all right, Doctor?" asked Zak.

"Maybe we should pray, Zak," said Ivy. "I read an article in a magazine. How plants grow bigger if you pray over them and when people pray, rays of light rise up toward heaven."

"Well, a little prayer wouldn't hurt," said Doctor Good. "Meanwhile, I'll see what I can do."

He began rooting through his knapsack. He pulled out a wooden mortar and pestle and poured in some dried herbs. He crushed them up and then added some flower petals from a little plastic baggie.

The children began to pray for their friend. Ziggy laid his head on Angelicus' chest. The jungle animals hung their heads in prayer, too. All the sounds of the rain forest stopped.

Doctor Good added water from his canteen to the herbs, roots and flowers. He was grinding away furiously, adding a little of this and a little of that. Finally he straightened up and poured the contents into a battered tin cup and brought it to the professor's lips.

"Doctor," asked Zak, "what is that stuff?"

"This mixture is something I learned from an old Indian woman. I'm giving him the essence of flowers. To balance his immune system. The cure for almost any known ailment can be found right here in the rain forest. It's in the flowers, the plants and bark of trees. We just have to know how to use them."

"You mean, like medicine?" asked Ivy.

"Yes," responded the doctor. "Now, let's see how this worked. What did you say his name was?"

"Professor Aquius Botanicus Angelicus," answered Zak.

"Professor Angelicus," called Doctor Good, "can you hear me?" He gave him a little more of the remedy and shook his arm.

The professor's ears twitched and his eyes blinked.

"It looks like he's coming to!" exclaimed the doctor. "It looks like he might be out of the woods!"

An aura of white light began to radiate from the professor's body. His ears perked up, turned bright green and a new yellow bud appeared at the top of his antenna. He opened one eye and then the other. At first, one was dark green and the other, deep blue. Gradually they came into focus and both turned a brilliant clear aquamarine. He blinked a few times.

"Oh my," the professor finally said, "have I missed the Rainbow Festival?"

Gales of laughter and cheers erupted through the forest clearing.

"Hooray, hooray! He's gonna be all right!" called out all the animals.

Ziggy barked and jumped up on his hind legs and danced around Angelicus with joy.

"Oh, Professor," said Ivy with relief, "you had us so worried!

Thank heavens the animals came. And the doctor with his flower essence. They saved your life!"

"Oh, I'm sorry," said Angelicus, "I didn't mean to worry you children." He looked at the botanist. "Are you the good doctor?"

"No, I'm Doctor Good. Doctor Dewing S. Good at your service, sir. You certainly were in sorry shape. You'd better have a little bit more of this." He raised the professor's head and gave him the last few drops of the tonic from the cup.

Angelicus' eyes began to sparkle and the bud on his antenna bloomed into a bright yellow flower. He looked lovingly at Zak and Ivy.

Ziggy furiously kissed his face.

"It's so good to know there are such true friends in the universe," he said, and looked at the creatures surrounding him. "And thank you, Ziggy. You're a brave little dog. And you, all my friends of the rain forest—you certainly were my Guardian Angels, saving my life and restoring my faith."

He scratched Ziggy on the ear.

The capybara said, "What good are friends if they can't help each other?"

"We all lose faith once in a while," purred Reiki the jaguar. "It's only natural."

The harpy eagle called down from the top of the kapok tree, "Yep! But you've just got to fly on through the highs and the lows, no matter what." He ruffled his wings and a feather floated down to land by the travelers' feet.

Zak picked it up and saved it for good luck. It looked just like one of the feathers hanging from the professor's pipe.

"Thank you, Professor," chimed in all the other jungle animals, "you saved our lives, too, by asking Daido to sing and make it rain."

Zak and Ivy smiled at each other. They knew they'd always be best friends.

Little Ziggy wagged his tail. He wondered what all the fuss was about. He knew what friends were for. After all, wasn't that one of his most important jobs here on Earth?

THE ICE WORLD

"**P**rofessor Angelicus," said Doctor Good, "the best thing for you is to get back to your home—to your own atmosphere. And as soon as possible."

"That's exactly where I plan to go," said Angelicus firmly, getting back on his feet, "as soon as we get to the Falls of the Angels and get some pure water."

The doctor looked shocked. "The Falls of the Angels? I wouldn't attempt that trip, Professor. I've been there. You'll run into more fires on your way up the river. You don't want to have a relapse."

"Professor," interjected Zak, "maybe we should just go straight to the cold continent. Popadopadon said we'd find pure water there."

"I think the young man's right," said Good, scratching his beard. "Maybe you should go south. It's ninety percent ice and that's where the planet stores most of its fresh water. I have friends working on the White Continent. Other scientists. They say there's ancient water . . . frozen there for millions of years. Some of it's bound to be pure."

"Wait a minute," said Angelicus, eyeing the river suspiciously. The water was running gray from ash and soot washed in by the storm. "I don't know if I can blow a sturdy enough bubble from that river water to get us anywhere."

"Yeah, it's probably very acid from the rain," said the doctor, picking up his canteen. "Maybe this water'll do the trick. It's distilled."

Doctor Good offered the canteen to Angelicus, who lifted the pipe. The sun was shining brightly in the sky. Its rays sparkled on the water as the doctor poured it into the bowl.

Good noticed the pipe. "Hey," he said, "your pipe, Professor. It reminds me of the ones I've seen up North. The natives where I come from call them peace pipes."

"Well," answered Angelicus, "I guess that's what you could call this one, too. Thank you, Doctor Good, for the water," he continued. "I think it'll do just fine. C'mon, kids. It seems we're going to the cold continent."

As Zak, Ivy and Ziggy came close, he took a deep breath and blew hard on the pipe. A bubble formed around them and they lifted up into the air.

"Goodbye, Reiki! Goodbye, Doctor Good! Goodbye, all you wonderful Sharelings of the rain forest!" they called.

Ziggy barked and wagged his tail.

"Now, you take it easy, Professor," called Doctor Good.

"Don't push yourself too hard. It's cold down there."

The animals all yelled, "Good luck, Professor! You'll find pure water! We know you will! Bye, Ivy! Bye, Zak! Bye, Ziggy!"

A warm tropical breeze blew from the west and Angelicus pushed the green button on the pipe.

The sky was heavy with air traffic. Two giant condors, flocks of migrating shorebirds, ducks and geese flew with them, wishing Angelicus and the children a safe trip south.

When the bubble got out over the open sea, Angelicus shifted gears on the pipe, and the wind started wailing from the north.

"Supersonic drive engaged," the pipe called out and with a BOOM like a jet plane, the bubble blasted southward.

"Professor," yelled Ivy, holding onto her rocking chair, "you'd better slow down. Remember what the doctor told you."

"Don't worry, I'm in top shape. I feel chipper now." His eyes were bright and clear and his ears stood up straight on his head. His flower antenna glowed like a hundred-watt light bulb.

"Way to go, Professor!" yelled Zak. "We'll be there in no time." He looked down at his watch. The hands weren't moving.

Ziggy barked, excited.

The green coast rapidly disappeared from sight. Soon, icebergs and scattered islands rose up from the deep blue ocean. Big white, fluffy clouds hung low in the sky. The brilliant light of the sun cast a blue glow from the reflections that bounced off the snowcapped rocky mountaintops. Gulls, petrels, terns and cormorants flew past the travelers, welcoming them to the White Continent.

"Hey," yelled Zak, "there's a colony of Adelie penguins!"

They could hear the chatter of thousands upon thousands

of red-eyed penguins perched on the rocks below the bubble.

A group of gigantic elephant seals were lying on the clean, sandy beach, belching and burping. Their pups were playing nearby.

"That must be Deception Island," said Zak. "Or is it Dream Island, Ivy? Remember when we studied it in geography?"

"I don't know," answered Ivy, "but look—there's Macaroni penguins!"

A rookery of Macaronis with their bright yellow crests were standing upright on the beach, like people dressed in tuxedos on their way to a ball. The birds looked up and waved hello.

The bubble passed by a boiling volcano steaming up into the frozen air. Then it traveled over a giant glacier that twisted and stretched its way down through a long valley to the rocky shores of a large bay.

Ivy looked down and saw a thousand bubbles in a perfect circle popping on the surface of the water. "Zak," she said, "those bubbles are being made by humpback whales!"

"What do you mean?" he asked.

"Don't you remember? In that movie? The humpbacks swim together in circles and they blow bubbles. It brings krill and all kinds of little fish into one place so the whales can eat them. Look—they're coming to the surface."

The elegant sea creatures breached gracefully one at a time. Plumes of water sprayed high into the air. Then, with a flip of their magnificent tails, the whales slipped back down to return to the hunt.

"Great bubble power, my friends!" Angelicus called down. He had a big, broad smile on his face, and his eyes were as blue as the sky.

As far as they could see, the breathtaking beauty of the mystical frozen White Continent stretched out before them.

"What a beautiful part of your planet this is!" Angelicus exclaimed. "It truly is a treasure. So white and sparkling clean and unspoiled. It looks like clear sailing from here on out, kids. I know we'll find the water we need."

Just as he said that, the weather abruptly changed. The sun disappeared into a dense fog that rapidly advanced on the bubble. Ziggy jumped into Zak's lap and tried to bury his nose under the boy's shirt.

"Professor," said Zak, "there must be a storm coming!"

"Hmm," said Angelicus, glancing at the little lights blinking on and off on the pipe, "Ziggy's right. The temperature is dropping drastically. It looks like we're in for a snowy ride. You'd better hold onto your chairs, kids. I'll put on some heat."

He pushed the yellow button twice and the pipe squawked, "Auxiliary heating activated."

A howling wind swept in from all directions and buckets of thick snow swirled around the bubble, tossing it and throwing it like a toy sailboat caught in a gale at sea. They could barely see from the snowflakes—each one a different shape and size—falling and splattering on the surface of the bubble.

"Yow," yelled Zak over the wail of the wind, "it's a blizzard!"

"Professor," shrieked Ivy, "maybe we should turn back!"

"Don't worry, Ivy," answered Angelicus, "we've just got to have faith. Stay focused and keep moving forward. Keep an eye on the future. There are always distractions and unexpected obstacles that pop up and get in the way . . . just last-minute details. We'll handle it."

"Last minute details?" Ivy responded. "You call a blizzard

a detail? I'm not losing faith, Professor. I'm just being practical . . ."

The professor blinked his eyes. "You're right, Ivy," he said. "There's faith and then there's "blind" faith. This is a pretty big storm. We should probably go down and wait it out. It might be tricky, but I think we can do it."

Angelicus closed his eyes and, with deep concentration, began delicately pushing forward on the controls, first to the left and then to the right. "Here we go," he said.

"Turbulence ahead. Icing conditions. Prepare for emergency instrument landing," announced the pipe. "Please return to your seats and fasten your seat belts."

"What seat belts?" asked Ivy.

Instantly, seat belts appeared at the sides of the children's chairs and securely fastened them in. A pair grew up out of Ziggy's rag rug and wrapped snugly around him.

They all held on for dear life as the bubble inched its way against the unbelievable force of the storm.

Soon they felt a soft bump. The bubble bounced on the ice and slid to a stop. For a moment the wind calmed, and they could see they had come to rest against the wall of a glacier.

"I don't know if the wind will stay calm for long," said the professor. "You know the wind—it's such a free spirit. It may want to wail again. In the meantime I think we'll build some shelter."

Zak asked, "How're you gonna do that, Professor?"

"Just watch," responded Angelicus. "All you need is cold air and a little water, and you can build almost anything."

He pushed on the blue button, then the white, and the blue again.

"Arm extending," called out the pipe, and the stem pushed out through the bubble's skin. The bowl transformed into a scoop like a front-end loader and began scooping up snow and packing it around the bubble. Zak and Ziggy watched, fascinated.

"Cool!" said Zak. "The pipe is making an igloo."

"And just in time—the wind is picking up again," said Angelicus.

The pipe scooped the last bit of snow onto the surface of the bubble and retracted into the craft, leaving a small doorway so the occupants could see out. "We'll be snug as a bug in here till the storm passes."

Through the doorway, they watched the storm. Eventually it let up and the sun broke through the clouds.

"It's time to go. We've got to find that water," said Angelicus. "But first, we're going to need protection from the cold. We need insulation. So I've got to transfer the skin of the bubble onto us."

Ivy asked, "How do you do that?"

"Remember," responded the professor with a grin, "a bubble can do almost anything."

First he slid the pipe up to the top of the bubble. Then he brought the tip to his mouth and, inhaling deeply, drew air in through the stem.

"Professor," said Zak, "the bubble has separated from the igloo. It's getting smaller."

"That's right," said Angelicus. "You don't want to be wearing that snow, do you?" He pushed on the orange button three times.

"Bubble suit maker in operation," called out the pipe, and

its bowl transformed into a bubble wand large enough to go around the children's bodies.

"Now," said the professor, "Zak, you first. Keep your arms at your sides and stand still."

Angelicus stretched the hoop down over Zak's head, bringing a little bit of the bubble with it. When he reached the boy's feet he pulled the wand free. With a pop, Zak was in his own private bubble. It shrank snugly around his body and left a bubble helmet around his head. He looked just like an astronaut.

"Supersonic!" yelled Zak, his voice muffled. "I feel warmer already."

The professor made a bubble suit for Ivy, then one for Ziggy, and finally, one for himself.

"OK, kids!" he exclaimed, sliding his pipe into the loop on his belt next to the empty bottle. "Now we can go find some pure water."

Suddenly they heard a noise on the outside wall of the igloo: "Tap, tap, taptap, tap, tap, taptap."

"What's that tapping?" Ivy asked.

"It sounds like someone wants to get in," said Angelicus. "Who's there?" he called.

A gravelly voice answered from outside. "It's Galanthus," it said, "Galanthus, king of the Emperor penguins."

"Well, come around to the front door," Angelicus directed him. "We can't see you where you are."

The professor wasn't taking any chances that Borrell had returned. They all went to the door to see who this Galanthus was.

Waddling around the edge of the igloo came an enormous penguin. He was as big as Zak and nearly as tall as the professor.

A lemon yellow breast and orange ear patches accented his chubby, torpedo-shaped, black and white body. A purple stripe ran the length of his long feathered beak and his sleek black wings hung almost to the ground.

"Come on in," said Angelicus.

The penguin barely squeezed through the opening. Ziggy sniffed the immense toenails of the penguin's large dark gray feet. He'd never seen a bird like this before—not one that stood upright like a human.

The penguin gave several quick bows to the occupants.

Angelicus solemnly returned the bow. "How do you do, Galanthus, Your Highness," he said. "Allow us to introduce ourselves. I'm—"

With another bow, the penguin interrupted: "I know who you are. At least I think I do. You're Professor Angelicus and Zak, Ivy, and Ziggy. Am I right?"

"Right you are," answered the professor.

"A little bird told me you'd be arriving," continued Galanthus. "A hawk. He flies almost to the rain forest to get food for his babies. He brought the news of your coming. Said you'd be here. But I didn't know you'd be so shiny. Welcome to the ice world."

"Pleased to meet you, Your Highness," said Angelicus.

"Aw, just call me Galanthus," said the penguin, shuffling his feet.

"Galanthus. Thank you for your warm welcome. We aren't normally so shiny but these are bubble suits—for protection from the cold."

Angelicus glanced around. "It's a little cramped in here. Why don't we all step outside for a little fresh air."

The penguin got caught trying to turn around in the doorway. He laughed. "Sorry about this. I just ate. My first meal in six months! I guess I forgot my size. I'm afraid I'm stuck."

The travelers smiled.

"Here," said Zak, "we'll help you."

They all began helping the penguin out of the doorway. They pushed and pulled and tried to turn him around until, finally, he popped out of the hole. He landed on his side in the snow. The children ran and helped him to his feet.

The awkward bird flapped his wings to clean off the snow.

"Clumsy of me," he said, and laughed again. "Anyway, I was told you were looking for pure water and thought maybe I could help."

"We most certainly are," said Angelicus. "We started at the river and have been to the bay. We've been under the sea and deep into the rain forest. All the Sharelings of your planet have tried to help us and we still haven't found it. If I can't find absolutely pure water here, I'll never get home to Quantia! We truly would be delighted with any help you could give us."

"Well," said Galanthus, "there's plenty of pure water here, but, as you can imagine, it's all frozen—and deep under the surface, as well. This stuff on the top is all right, but I wouldn't guess it to be pure. It's been almost everywhere on the planet, picking up foreign substances . . . not natural to its nature."

"If it's under the surface, that might not be a problem," Angelicus responded. "My pipe can do a lot of things. Where do you think our best chances would be of finding the purest water, Galanthus?"

"Well," responded the penguin, "I'd say Paradise Bay. That's where the rest of my flock is waiting out the spring thaw. We've just finished keeping last winter's babies warm through the dark months and now we're getting ready to head out for our yearly migration north on the ice floes. I can point out a few likely spots."

"Well, I guess we'd best get going," said Angelicus.

The green-eared alien, the two children, and the little white dog set off briskly in their bubble suits and helmets, following the stately penguin across the glistening snow.

"Professor," exclaimed Ivy in awe, "how beautiful it is here!"

The white world shimmered.

"This must be what Quantia's like, huh, Professor?" Zak asked.

"It does have a lot of the same sparkle, Zak. It does feel like I'm getting closer to home."

Up ahead, stretched out across the peaceful horizon, they could see a colony of penguins walking in single file.

Ivy asked, "Is that your flock, Galanthus?"

"That's them." The penguin quickened his pace. "Would you like to meet the family?"

They caught up with Galanthus' flock and were suddenly surrounded by hundreds of chattering penguins. The children laughed delightedly as a fuzzy young penguin with light gray feathers and a black and white face raced clumsily up to Galanthus and nuzzled close.

"This is my new daughter, Snow Drop," said the proud father. "She was born just this year. And this is my wife, Isis."

The adult penguin following the baby stopped and bowed.

"How do you do, Isis and Snow Drop," said Angelicus.

They all bowed back. Ziggy ran up to the young penguin and tried to give her a kiss, but his bubble helmet got in the way.

CHAPTER FIFTEEN

They were traveling across a flat area between two gigantic, blue ice sculptures that rose high into the air. The snow had blown away, exposing the smooth ice under their feet.

Galanthus stopped and turned. "This might be a good spot to check, Professor," he said. "Professor?"

Angelicus was staring up at the sky, his eyes very large. "Galanthus," he called out in alarm, "a piece of the sky is missing! There's a hole in the sky!"

The penguin nodded. "I'm glad you noticed that, Professor," he said. "That hole showed up a few years ago. We think it has something to do with all the little tiny plants—the plankton—disappearing from the water. The shrimp and fish eat it. Without the fish, we won't have anything to eat ourselves."

"You can see the ozone hole?" asked Zak.

"Certainly," answered Angelicus. "Look. Look there. It's definitely a different color. It's darker. Isn't that the hole you told me about in the rain forest, Zak? What caused it?"

"They say it's from chemicals we put into the air," said Zak. "Freon."

"From hair spray and refrigerators," added Ivy.

The professor shook his head. "No wonder Daido and his friends' eggs aren't hatching!" he exclaimed. "That ozone is part of your Big Blue Ball's immune system. It's a protective layer. It keeps damaging light waves from getting through to the surface. Every Shareling on your planet depends on it. Can't the Guardian Residents see that? Holes don't just let things out, they let things in."

They were all staring up at the hole in the sky when Ziggy growled.

"Is that another bubble up there?" asked Galanthus.

They heard the shrill wailing of a police siren and a bubble raced down toward them from the ozone hole.

As it got closer, Ivy caught a glimpse of the driver, who looked just like a black and white version of Angelicus.

"Is that someone from Quantia, Professor," she asked, "coming to get you—to bring you home?"

Ziggy didn't think so. It didn't smell right to him. He had smelled that smell before—on the river—at the bay—under the ocean—and in the rain forest. He looked up at Angelicus. The professor's eyes were glazed over and all four of his ears were standing straight up on his head, shaking.

The alien bubble careered down and swirled directly over them. Then it smacked Zak on the side of his helmet and the boy was sucked up into the craft. Ziggy jumped up and tried to pull Zak back. His bubble suit popped and he joined his best friend. They both looked down helplessly as the bubble rose.

The professor fell to his knees, the weight of the world on his shoulders. "Oh, my starry nights, what have I done? It's all my fault!"

"That's Borrell, isn't it?" Ivy screamed.

The intruder shouted demonically over the wailing sirens: "Hah! Yeah, it is your fault—you failed! You're a fraud! Where are your beautiful thoughts now, Angelicus? Can't think? Your failure get in the way? You got no advice for yourself, blabbermouth?" Its blank eyes stared coldly at the gathering on the ice. "Go ahead—tell them. You were too late for Nega, weren't you? Too busy lecturing! What do you have now? I have your Earthlings—and this is just the beginning! Ha ha ha." He laughed maniacally and spun the bubble around and around. "Oh, boo-hoo. What'll you tell the Grand Council now?"

"Don't you talk to the professor like that, you maniac," Zak yelled.

He tried to wrestle the pipe free from the black and white creature, but it felt like he was wrestling with thin air. Ziggy bit Borrell's leg, but his teeth went right through as if he wasn't even there.

"Hah! You can't touch me, little boy, I'm not your nightmare." The creature said snidely, "I'm Borrell—Professor Borrellius—of the universe!" He pulled back on his pipe and the bubble whisked up and away. He looped around one of the ice sculptures and swooped low over the penguins, laughing like a hyena.

Ivy screamed, "Professor, get up! We've got to save Zak and Ziggy!" She reached over and grabbed him by the shoulder. In an instant, their suits merged to form a new bubble around them. "Will you please just stand up? Oh, what is wrong with you?"

Angelicus mumbled under his breath, "I failed, Ivy. I got there too late."

"What are you talking about?"

"Nega. Nega," he moaned.

"Oh, just give me the pipe!" She grabbed the pipe from his belt. "How does this thing work?"

"Just push the green button. Think of where you want to go, and pull back," Angelicus answered weakly. He rose shakily from his knees.

"Well then, hold on," yelled Ivy. She yanked back on the pipe.

A gale rose up around the bubble and they sailed toward Borrell and his prisoners.

Borrell laughed and took off, Ivy in hot pursuit. Around one ice sculpture they chased, across the barren plain, around the second, and back over the heads of the penguins, spinning and spinning—faster and faster. The wind engines raised up a blinding snow squall, forcing the penguins to bunch together.

As they traveled faster Ivy noticed that their bubble was rippling in the wind.

"Professor, what's wrong with the bubble? Is the bubble in trouble?" she asked.

"It must be that distilled water—it's clean but not as strong as it could be," Angelicus answered.

Borrell let out an evil laugh and yelled out, "Catch me if you can," and then slammed directly into them.

BOOM! Their bubble burst, and Ivy and Angelicus were thrown by the blast. Ivy, still gripping the pipe, fell to the icy snow among the penguins. The professor landed about fifty feet away.

Galanthus raced to save him and the other penguins moved in closely around Ivy so she wouldn't freeze. Ivy was looking around, dazed, when the pipe thundered and began vibrating in her hand. All the colored lights were flashing and racing up and down the stem.

"Bingo! Yahoo! Bravo!" the pipe yelled out. "Eureka! Outtasight! One hundred percent pure! H_2O! Aqua! Agua fresca! Water! Jackpot!"

"Professor," Ivy screamed out. "Professor—the pipe has found water! Come quick!"

Borrell raced down and screeched to a halt, hovering overhead.

Galanthus had taken the professor under his wing to keep

him warm. Angelicus' green ears and flower antenna perked straight up when he heard Ivy's call and he raced to the group. Galanthus waddled up behind.

"I'll do it, I'll do it," exclaimed Angelicus, and ran to relieve Ivy of the pipe.

"But what about Zak and Ziggy?" Ivy looked up at her captive friends in the bubble. "What about them?"

"Don't worry about us, Ivy," Zak yelled down. "Get the water!"

"How far down is the water?" Ivy asked.

"I don't know for sure," answered Angelicus. "That's the pipe's job."

"HAH! You fraud, Angelicus! You weed," Borrell yelled down in his venomous voice. "You'll never get that water. You'll never get home. No Rainbow Festival for you, pal."

"Hey," yelled Zak, "you shut up! Don't you dare talk to the professor like that!"

"Wruff," Ziggy agreed.

"You're not a fraud, are you, Professor?" asked Ivy.

Borrell yelled down again: "Tell them, you phony! You were too late to Nega—you wasted time helping someone else on your way there. Tell them, Angelicus—that you brought me here to the Big Blue Ball with you! Did you tell them that?"

"Ooh . . . he's right, Ivy. I was late to Nega—far too late. I failed. I lost millions. And Borrell did follow me here. Oh, I've let down the whole universe! I didn't do my job. I don't even deserve this pipe. I'm no planetary healer." He handed the pipe to Ivy. His ears hung limply in front of his face, his eyes a dark, cloudy blue.

"Professor, you mean Borrell is here because of you? You

have negative thoughts and fears?"

"Yes." The sensitive creature nodded sadly. "And I haven't been honest with myself, and I haven't been totally honest with you children, either."

"But . . . but didn't you do all that you could do to save the Negans?"

"Well, yes."

"And didn't you stop to help another Shareling on your way to Nega?" She put her hand on his shoulder.

Angelicus nodded, his eyes beginning to clear.

"Well what's wrong with that? Nobody's perfect. You're only human—I mean alien."

"I'm just a tiny, teeny speck in the universe," Angelicus acknowledged. His green ears twitched.

"And what about everything you've shared with us? You've taught us so much!" Ivy reminded him. "You're not responsible for a whole planet, Professor. You did the best that you could do. You've got to forgive yourself." She gently stroked his left lower ear. "And we've found the water—and the water will take you home to Quantia. Think of the Rainbow Festival!"

Angelicus' eyes turned soft blue and slowly lit up. "You're right, Ivy. Great galloping galaxies, what a fool I've been! I didn't practice what I preached. I did blame myself—and let Borrell in."

His ears stood up straight and his flower antenna rotated. "It's true. I did do the best that I could do."

"Way to go, Professor!" cheered Zak from above. He turned to Borrell. "You big bully, you wait and see what happens to you!" he sneered.

Ziggy sniffed and lifted his leg on the creature.

Borrell began to shrink and to fade . . . paler and paler.

"Drilling unit activated," called out the pipe. The bowl turned into a drill bit and the pipe stretched into a long coil of thin tubing. The tip began to glow and spin very fast. Humming loudly, it burrowed into the ice.

"Put the pipe to your ear and listen," said Angelicus.

Ivy put the pipe to her ear. "What am I listening for?"

"Why—water."

"Well, I hear something." She pulled the pipe from her ear and, echoing up through the stem came the sound of a huge roar of applause and the voices of a billion people cheering.

"Aargh!" Borrell let out a gurgle of frustrated rage.

Angelicus pulled the water bottle from his belt and unscrewed the lid. A roll of drums sounded and then the music of a brass marching band blared from the mouthpiece.

"Stand back," he said. His eyes turned a bright golden color and he held the pipe at arm's length.

At first a tiny trickle of water appeared at the mouthpiece, sputtering and spitting.

Angelicus muttered, "There's air in the line."

Soon, water began to flow freely through the stem of the pipe. The more it flowed the more it sparkled. The more it sparkled the faster it flowed. Finally, with an incredible roar, warm, steaming crystal-clear water erupted like a geyser. High into the sky it went, spraying over Borrell's bubble. The craft slowly descended to the ground and evaporated, leaving Zak and Ziggy standing with the professor, Ivy, and the penguins. Borrell was nowhere to be seen.

"Oh my goodness!" exclaimed Angelicus. "This is more than I could have ever hoped for! More than I could have ever imagined or dreamed up. This is a miracle!"

His eyes filled up with tears of joy. They looked like two swirling, twinkling rainbows. The flower on his antenna was shining like the sun on a hot summer afternoon and his four green ears stretched out excitedly as he cocked his head and listened to the drops of water gently falling.

"This water is very wise and clear. It's truly sacred. Purer than pure! Look, kids, each one of these tiny drops remembers the beginning of creation. Listen. The water speaks the truth. The pipe must have gone to the very core of your Big Blue Ball!"

With a huge smile on his face and a sparkle in his eyes, he held the bottle out to catch the steaming water flowing from the pipe. "Take the bottle, Zak, and put the lid on for me, will you?" he asked.

Zak proudly stepped forward, took the shimmering bottle and carefully screwed the lid down tight. Ivy, Ziggy and the penguins pressed in close to get a look. Zak held it out for them to see.

The professor pushed the red and yellow buttons on the pipe, and the voice called faintly.

"Drilling complete. Deactivating," it said. The pipe shrank back to its original shape.

"Well," the professor said, "mission accomplished!"

He looked lovingly around at the flock of penguins and Ivy, Zak, and Ziggy.

"What a great gift you of the Big Blue Ball have given me," he said reverently. "You've given me the way to go home—a way to recognize the good in myself—even at the worst of times. How can I ever thank all the Sharelings of this planet? But we really must be going. 'Cause it looks like the sun will be setting and we've got to catch the sparkle while it's here."

"We understand, Professor," said Galanthus. "The spring thaw is almost over. The ice'll break soon and we'll be heading north ourselves. We've got to catch the moment while we can. We hope you'll come back and visit us soon. And you too, Ziggy, Zak, and Ivy."

He turned to face the rest of his flock. "The ice is breaking. We've got to be ready!" he said urgently.

The penguins quickly waddled away and huddled together at the edge of the water—just in time to hear the giant BOOM of cracking ice. The sound echoed through the ice shelf and bounced off the mountains of the white world. The area the penguins were standing on broke free and the humanoid birds floated away on a white, frozen raft of ice.

"Wow," said Ivy, "I guess Mother Nature told them it was time to go!"

"That's really cool!" said Zak.

"Goodbye, Professor. Goodbye, children. Goodbye, Ziggy," the penguins called as they slowly drifted out into the bay.

"Thank you again for your help, Galanthus," Angelicus responded. "Thanks for keeping us warm."

The children waved and called out, "Bye, Galanthus. Bye." Ziggy barked.

Angelicus took the crystal-clear water from Zak's hand and gingerly unscrewed the lid. He put one little drop of the sacred sparkling water into the pipe. The gold, silver and copper medallion on the professor's belt let out a huge clap of thunder and a brilliant burst of light. The children jumped back.

Angelicus threw his head back and laughed uproariously. "I was beginning to wonder if I would *ever* hear that sound again!"

he exclaimed. "It's almost too good to be true. It's time to head home to Quantia."

"Ahh . . . Professor," asked Ivy, "are you going to take us home first?"

"Home?" Angelicus roared. "Home? Don't you children want to see the Rainbow Festival? It only happens once every billion years!"

A dazed look came over the children's faces.

"Why . . . you would take us with you?" asked Ivy.

Ziggy wagged his tail and jumped up and down. He wanted to go to Quantia, for sure!

"Of course!" said Angelicus. His ears were standing straight up from his head and his eyes were lavender blue. "I wouldn't be going without you. I wouldn't have it any other way. After all, the festival wouldn't be the same if I didn't have my friends there to share it with. And you have been true Sharelings to me."

The children were speechless for a minute, then Zak suddenly remembered. "Professor," he said sadly, "I can't go. I've got to be home in time for dinner. At six o'clock." He hung his head.

Angelicus gave a gentle chuckle. "Zak," he said softly, "you'll be home in time for your dinner. I'd never want your parents to worry. You have my solemn oath. Remember we're in Bubble Time—and now we have plenty of Bubble Time!"

Zak's eyes lit up. "Yes!" he exclaimed.

Ziggy barked. He was looking forward to meeting his new friends on Quantia. He had known all along they would find the water.

The sun had a halo around it as it set into peach, pink and lavender blue clouds. A full moon was rising and ribbons of flashing light from an aurora were streaking across the sky, painting the incredible world of ice with pale, luminescent colors. Lemon yellow, green, and soft orange reflected from the snow and the water of the bay. They could hear the tinkling of shimmering ice crystals forming in the air as it cooled. A wandering albatross flew south. A giant white petrel headed west. A tern winged to the north and a snowy sheathbill, like a white dove, flew east.

In the mystical, magical moment, the professor closed his eyes and bowed his head. As he brought the pipe to his mouth, the three feathers hanging from the bowl fluttered in the gentle breeze. He took a deep, deep breath and blew a bubble. Rainbows raced across the surface of its skin.

"All right, children," he said softly, "the time is now. Just walk close to the bubble. The bubble will take care of the rest."

The children and Ziggy slowly approached the awesome-colored bubble. It expanded around them and in an instant they were all standing on the invisible floor. The children's chairs appeared, Ziggy's rug was crumpled up just as he had left it, and Angelicus stood ready at the controls.

"Now children, Ziggy," Angelicus said, "we must all concentrate very deeply. There's a little ice flower just to the right, there. Do you see it?"

A beautiful ice crystal was floating on the water of the bay. The sun's setting rays reflected from its surface.

"I see it," said Ivy.

"Me too," affirmed Zak.

Ziggy barked.

A gentle breeze stirred in the frozen air and the bubble floated toward the dazzling ice crystal.

"OK," said the professor. "Now, look only at that sparkle. Allow your spirits to join with the light. Be the light. That sparkle is our path to Quantia. Get ready, kids. This bubble is going to the center of the universe."

The children stared into the brilliant, shimmering ice crystal. The energy of its white rays surrounded and cradled them and every color of the rainbow flashed before their eyes. A sweet smell filled the air.

"Zak," whispered Ivy, "I see angels!"

"I do too, Ivy," breathed Zak.

"Those are the guides on our journey," intoned Angelicus. "Let them carry you."

They could feel a warm, tranquil, harmonious light bursting and radiating from deep inside their hearts and souls. Their bodies and minds seemed to gently fall away and their spirits rose up and merged with the swirling liquid rainbow light of the bubble as they began to enter the crystal. Somehow, somewhere they remembered having this wondrous feeling before.

Ziggy remembered this feeling, too. "Have I ever gone to Quantia before?" the little dog wondered.

The bubble's light merged with the light from the crystal and the four friends were on their way to the Rainbow Festival.

CHAPTER SIXTEEN

THE LAND OF SPARKLE AND THE RAINBOW FESTIVAL

Everything was pitch black. There was no light from the pipe; no sparkle from the professor's eyes; even the lighted dial on Zak's watch was dark.

"Where are we, Professor?" asked Zak.

"We're in the corridor of white light. We're riding the rays of the Great Starpath," responded Angelicus.

Ivy was confused. "Then why can't I see anything?" she asked.

"It's part of the path," said Angelicus. "Without darkness there can be no light. They're always connected. There is day and night everywhere in the universe, just like on your Big Blue Ball. Think of all the wonderful things that happen at night . . . the owl hoots, the frogs sing and the bats fly. And besides, if you didn't have the night you couldn't see the stars. Look straight ahead and concentrate. You'll see the light."

Soon enough, the teeniest pinpoint of light appeared in the deep blackness . . . then another . . . and another. The points grew larger and larger like the headlights of cars on a wet road at night, piercing through the darkness. The beams of light streamed across space.

"Look, Zak," exclaimed Ivy, "they look like roads in space! And they're all coming together at a big tree. A weeping willow tree. And there's a big golden gate on the trunk of the tree."

"Is that where we're going, Professor?" asked Zak.

"That's where we're going," answered Angelicus. "That's the gate to Quantia."

"Where do all those roads come from, Professor?" asked Ivy.

"They come from everywhere in the universe," he answered, "and all the roads of light lead to the same place. You see? Our road is no different than any other. It still winds up at the gate."

Sure enough, the children saw that the bubble was traveling on one of the pathways. It was moving faster and faster and, as they got closer, they had a better view of the willow. The tree was standing in the middle of a grassy knoll on a large rock that was floating in space and it looked like it had been carved from gemstones. The willow glistened like a jewel. It had a golden brown topaz trunk, yellow crystal leaves and the glowing golden gate on the tree trunk was shaped like a heart.

The lights on the pipe started blinking. "Approaching Quantia. Approaching home field," it called out. "It's a beautiful night out there, folks. We've got clear, clear skies ahead and a smooth landing. Prepare for final destination."

In no time at all the bubble landed onto a soft, cushiony field and rolled up to the tree. It gently popped and the children, Ziggy and Angelicus were all lying on the grass.

Ivy ran her fingers through the lush lawn and sighed, "This grass feels like velvet!"

Ziggy rolled around in the glittering dewdrops.

A rosebush was climbing all over the golden gate. Each sweet-smelling blossom was a different color of the rainbow, and each was making a musical sound all its own.

"Look how many stars there are," said Ivy. "There are billions of them. And they're all twinkling a different color."

"Those aren't just stars you're seeing, Ivy," said Angelicus with a smile. "From here, we can see every planet in the universe."

"Is this Quantia, Professor?" asked Zak.

"Almost," he answered. "Almost. This is one of our moons. Through the gate and down the Rainbow Bridge and we'll be there."

Zak walked up to the gate and rattled a golden bar. "There's no latch on this gate. There's no way to open it. How do we get through?"

"We have to follow our hearts and just ask," answered Angelicus. "Before it will open, we must leave all of our bad dreams behind. We better get a move on. There will be others landing pretty soon. We have to leave room for them."

On the pathways crisscrossing the sky, hundreds of bubbles were approaching. They were all different colors and sizes and they were all heading toward the gate.

"Professor," Zak asked, "where are they coming from?"

"From all over the universe," answered Angelicus. "They're all coming to the Rainbow Festival, so we must hurry. Just follow me and do what I do—one at a time."

Angelicus walked up to the heart-shaped gate in the trunk of the tree and called out, "I'd like to go onto Quantia. Please let me in."

A huge rumbling voice came from the tree: "You may not bring any bad dreams with you into the Land of Sparkle. Have you left them all behind?"

"I have," answered Angelicus.

"Then enter," it said, "and welcome!"

The golden heart swung open, just enough to let the professor through. It quickly swung shut behind him, leaving the children and Ziggy alone on the grass.

"Zak," hissed Ivy, "you go next."

"No. You go ahead, Ivy," answered Zak.

Ziggy ignored them. He couldn't wait to go to Quantia and make new friends. He ran up to the gate and barked twice. The gate barked back at him and Ziggy answered with a "Woof! I have."

Once again the heart opened and quickly shut.

"Come on, Ivy," said Zak.

He took hold of her hand and, after answering the question together, they proceeded through the gate.

Angelicus and Ziggy were waiting for them by a long, rainbow-colored pathway that spiraled downward.

"Are we gonna walk?" asked Ivy. "It looks like a hundred miles!"

The professor laughed. "No, we're going to slide. We call it a bridge but on your Big Blue Ball I think you'd call it a sliding board."

With that, he stepped onto the Rainbow Bridge, let out a whoop and, like a skier without skies, slid down and out of sight.

One at a time the children and Ziggy followed the professor onto the bridge. Zak and Ivy stood up straight and stretched their arms out at their sides. Their hair flew back as they careered downward, screaming with joy. Ziggy planted his feet forward on the slide, his tongue hanging out of the side of his mouth, and his fur was flying.

They slid down the Rainbow Bridge, faster and faster. As they were catching up to the professor, they saw, to their astonished horror, that the slide was coming to an end—right into the mouth of a dragon!

"Whoa!" yelled Zak and leaned back, trying to slow down. Ivy screamed and Ziggy yipped, trying to turn around and run back up the slide. His feet spun under him.

Not only was the dragon's mouth immense, but it had huge, pointy teeth, fiery red eyes, a scaly pink and turquoise body that went on for a mile, and gigantic wings flapping up and down. It was puffing purple smoke from its flaring nostrils.

Angelicus let out a hearty laugh and yelled, "Here we come, Karmapa, ready or not!"

They heard a bellow of greeting come from deep inside the dragon's belly and they all slid in over the serpent's great forked tongue. They were instantly bathed in an orange light that glowed from the inner walls of the monstrous dragon's body.

"Professor," yelled Ivy, "what is this all about?"

"This is Karmapa, the Guardian of the Gate and the last checkpoint for Borrell. We ride through him to slow down—all the way through his body and out the tip of his tail. Isn't it wonderful? Although I understand it wouldn't be so nice for someone who hasn't left his fears behind!" He let out another hearty laugh.

Soon the passageway grew smaller and a ray of light poured in through a crack in Karmapa's tail. The crack opened wider and the children, Ziggy and Angelicus slid out into the Land of Sparkle!

The children found themselves in the most beautiful, magical, wondrous land they had ever seen! Two suns hung in a rainbow-colored sky, one in the east and one in the west. They were shining down on a quaint little village that lay nestled in a magical, sparkling valley. Flocks and flocks of birds flew through fluffy marshmallow clouds that drifted above the mountaintops.

One majestic, glistening, white mountain stood much higher than the rest. They couldn't even see the peak. It disappeared into the mist. Cascading down over its shimmering cliffs was a rainbow-colored waterfall. It glittered like diamonds, emeralds, rubies and sapphires in the light of the Quantian suns. Foamy bubbles tumbled down the waterfall, then rose up into the air and floated out over the fairy-tale landscape.

"Gee, Professor," said Ivy breathlessly, "this is the most beautiful place I have ever seen! This really *is* the Land of Sparkle!"

"Yeah," said Zak, "this is extremely excellent! Sixteen point seven million colors—right, Professor?"

"That's right," Angelicus said with a big grin. Every color of the rainbow twinkled in his eyes.

The air was filled with the sound of bells. They were ringing, tinkling, chiming and jingling like church bells, sleigh bells, wind chimes and temple bells.

"Professor, I hear bells," said Ivy.

"It's the rocks, Ivy," he answered, "the ringing rocks of Great Spirit Mountain." He pointed toward the mystical white mountain in the distance, his green ears standing straight up on his head and his flower antenna glowing. "The rainbow water of the Waterfall of Dreams pours down Great Spirit Mountain. And as it splashes over the ringing rocks, each drop of water makes a musical note all its own. When the wind on the mountain changes, so does the melody from the falls."

"I can't see the top," said Zak. "How high is Great Spirit Mountain, Professor?"

"No one knows for sure, Zak," answered Angelicus. "As high as you care to climb. I felt energetic once and decided to climb it, myself. I reached the forty-ninth level on the mountain. The journey took me fifty-one years, three months and twenty-six days, Earth time. But I saw no sign of the peak from there."

"You climbed for fifty-one years?" gasped Zak. "How did you do that? Didn't you get tired?"

"Sure I did," answered the professor, "but seeking the truth gives you the strength to keep going, no matter what. I just had to dig down deep inside myself. To my heart and soul. Do my homework, so to speak. And then I took one step at a time. Anyone can do it, if they're willing to try. As a matter of fact, everyone on the Grand Council has climbed to at least fifty-five levels. They say that the peak of the mountain is the home of the Great Universal Source. Nobody I know has ever been there. It just goes up and up and up."

Zak said, "I'd like to climb that mountain."

"Me too," said Ivy.

"In a way, you've already started to, Zak and Ivy."

"We have?" asked the children.

"Sure you have," answered Angelicus. "You've already taken

your first steps. I never would have found that sparkling water on the Big Blue Ball if you hadn't been such true Sharelings and come with me. You showed great faith, courage and love. They're the first steps. One day you'll climb that mountain, Zak and Ivy. Maybe we'll climb it together, and I hope you go higher than fifty-five levels."

Ziggy barked. He wanted to climb the mountain, too.

"And you too, Ziggy." Angelicus laughed. "But first things first. We don't want to miss the Rainbow Festival. This way, kids."

A signpost with an arrow read Point Pleasant. It pointed down a flower-lined path that led into the valley. The travelers followed it toward the little village below.

A babbling blue creek ran by the side of the velvet green path on its way to the crystal-clear river in the distance. Hundreds of butterflies fluttered along with the children and Ziggy, welcoming them to the Land of Sparkle.

The children's feet felt so light they barely touched the ground.

"It feels like I'm walking on air," Ivy observed.

"We only use gravity when we need it, here on Quantia," said Angelicus.

They rounded a curve in the path and two small, aquamarine-eyed Quantians ran toward them.

"Uncle Aquius," called out the taller of the two. The little Quantian looked very much like the professor, but he had four yellow ears and a short antenna topped with a bright red flower.

"Children," called out the professor, joyfully running to hug the two, "you've come to meet us!"

"Of course we've come!" called the smaller one. She was

clearly a young Quantian girl. Her ears were pink with green edges and the flower on her antenna looked like a blue morning glory. "The festival is starting. We were so worried you wouldn't get here!"

Angelicus smiled. "You know I wouldn't miss the Rainbow Festival for all the stars in the universe! But I've forgotten my manners. Harmonia and Orto, I'd like you to meet Zak, Ivy, and Ziggy. They've come with me from the Big Blue Ball. They helped me find the water my pipe needed to get me home. They are true Sharelings of the highest degree!"

"It's nice to meet you," said the young Quantians. "Thank you for bringing Uncle Aquius home."

They shook hands with Zak and Ivy. Ziggy put his paw up. He shook, too.

"There will be lots of games at the festival," said Harmonia. "Maybe the three of you would like to play. They're gonna be great!"

"Super!" said Zak.

"That sounds like fun," said Ivy. "What kind of games?"

"There'll be hopping and swimming and running. All sorts of games," answered Harmonia.

"But we've got to hurry," Orto said, "the flying games are first. And they're my favorite."

Ziggy barked and jumped up and down. He loved playing games—particularly ball games.

The four children and the dog turned and raced down the path toward the village. Angelicus followed behind.

The path ended in a big sunlit, central square. It looked like a huge flea market or carnival. Joyful music filled the air and in the center of the square was a large stone fountain. It was spouting crystal-clear water, and rainbow-colored bubbles were rising up from it and floating out over the crowd. There were hundreds of booths and tents and all kinds of unusual structures, big and small. There were strange crafts and odd-looking food, magic shows, and all sorts of things to tickle the imagination.

The crowd was made up of the most improbable-looking characters! Of course there were Quantians. Thousands of them! They all looked very much like the professor; they were dressed in rainbow clothes and each one's eyes and antenna were a different color. But the Quantians appeared ordinary to the children, compared to the other creatures in the crowd, who were walking (or not walking) around. There were purple people with six arms; and silver creatures the shape of balls that moved around by bouncing from place to place; and there were green stick beings hovering in the air, bending over the tables in the square and speaking to each other in high-pitched whistles!

And it wasn't just the visitors who were unusual. One booth was actually a huge hive and inside were a bunch of bees the size of grown men! They were handing out honey to everyone . . . and everything . . . that went by. The shiny rainbow tent next door was fluttering in the breeze and seemed to be growing by the minute. Inside it, giant light green worms were spinning silk like mad and tearing off pieces of the tent for anyone who asked.

"Where are all these guys from?" asked Zak.

"They're from everywhere," Harmonia said, laughing. "See that Shareling?"

She pointed at a creature that seemed spun from pink cotton candy. Zak and Ivy couldn't believe their eyes. The being was shifting back and forth from visible to invisible while they watched.

"She's from the Pink Ball," Harmonia said, "and those over there are from the Purple Ball, and there's a Shareling from the Yellow Ball."

"They're from many different galaxies," Orto added. "There are representatives here from all over the universe."

"Some of these Sharelings are terrific looking!" said Zak. He started walking toward the other booths. He couldn't wait to see what surprises they had in store.

"Zak," Orto called, "we can see the crafts later. The games are starting. This way."

They hurried out of the square, running past brightly paint-ed cottages and over a little bridge, down toward the river. A large rainbow-striped banner, waving overhead, read To the Games.

They turned a corner and came upon a split rail fence with wild honeysuckle climbing all over it, and Queen Anne's lace. The flowers were singing a song. Through an opening in the fence, the children could see rows and rows of trees, swaying in time to the music. There were plum trees with amethyst trunks and lavender leaves, and apple trees with ruby trunks and emer-ald leaves . . . fruit trees of every kind. From time to time the strong, swaying branches reached down and stroked the baby trees growing beneath them. The little seedlings were cooing and calling.

"Harmonia," Ivy asked in a hushed voice, "what is this place?"

"This is the nursery," answered the young Quantian.

"The trees will be sharing their fruit later," said Orto. "You can eat from every one of them, if you want. We can stop back after the games."

Past the fence they came out onto a huge, flat meadow lined

with bleachers made up of living branches and twigs—the games field.

The crowd was immense! Visitors from all over the universe were filling the bleachers to capacity. At one end of the field was a row of giant trees, which led to the banks of the river. There were thousands of birds on the branches, waiting for the flying games.

"This way!" yelled Orto.

In no time they were standing, lined up to play in the first event.

"Orto," asked Zak, "are you gonna fly?"

"Of course," responded Orto, "aren't you?"

"We can't fly," answered the boy, "not without airplanes or balloons or something."

"We heard that some Sharelings can't fly on their home planet," said Harmonia, "except at night, in their dreams. But anyone can fly on Quantia!"

"Are you sure?" asked Ivy. "Everybody? How?"

"Well," answered the young Quantian, "you just stop thinking about standing on the ground."

It made perfect sense to Ziggy. He'd always wanted to fly like his friends, the birds. So he followed Harmonia's instructions. He thought about being in the air and suddenly he was floating up by Zak's face.

"Wait, Ziggy," hissed Orto, "we have to wait for the crow to call."

Ivy and Zak practiced not standing on the ground till finally, a crow called out loud and clear from the top of a giant old ash tree.

"Caw! Caw, caw," it called. "It's time for the flying games to begin. Is the first group ready?"

"That's us," said Orto, and they all answered, "Ready!"

"Then fly," called the crow.

Ivy and Zak stretched their arms out at their sides and began to rise into the air. Ziggy pointed his tail straight back and bounded skyward. The five friends joined hundreds of others gleefully flying in the space above the field.

All sorts of animals . . . frogs, deer, salamanders, squirrels; bizarre-looking intergalactic creatures; giant insects; Quantians of every color; and of course, birds of all shapes and sizes flew by.

"Ivy," yelled Zak, "don't you love this? Don't you love flying?"

"Yeah!" exclaimed Ivy, laughing. "I always wished I had wings and could fly." She swooped away, avoiding a close call with a flying turtle. "Bet you can't catch me, Zak," she called over her shoulder.

The children, Ziggy, and their new friends glided out over the sparkling river. A fish jumped and flew into the air. Ziggy dove down to play with it and they both soared up into the trees. Ziggy wanted to try other things birds could do, so he settled down awkwardly on one of the high pine branches. He swayed back and forth, fighting to keep his balance, and the fish joined him.

Ziggy couldn't wait to tell his friends on Earth about the flying games. This was a lot more fun than chasing Frisbees.

"Hey, Ziggy," called Orto, flying by, "these are the flying games. Not the perching games—they're later."

Ziggy and the fish quickly flew back to the group.

Zak stretched the palms of his hands upward, opened his

fingers wide and caught a rising air current. Higher and higher he circled, Ivy following.

"I feel like a turkey buzzard!" Zak exclaimed.

"I feel like I'm in heaven," sighed Ivy.

Zak could see everything on the ground as clearly as if it were right in front of him. "I guess this is what having an 'eagle eye' means," he thought to himself.

Harmonia and Orto joined them, and Orto called out, "We should be getting back. Our turn is almost over."

They soared up along a cliff and took one spin around the base of Great Spirit Mountain. The wind was calm and the bells from the Ringing Rocks jingled softly. The four friends held hands and floated through the rainbow bubbles rising up from the Waterfall of Dreams. The bubbles popped and they could feel the spray on their faces.

"It feels like the fizz from a soda," said Ivy.

"What's soda?" asked Orto.

Ivy answered, "If you ever come visit us on Earth, you'll have some. You'll love it!"

They headed back down to the field. Ziggy and the fish raced to join them just as the crow called out again.

"Caw, caw, caw," it sang out, "first group, your time is done."

The fish dropped back into the river and the five friends settled into their final descent. Zak spotted Professor Angelicus in the bleachers with a group of the cotton candy visitors from the Pink Ball. With a big broad smile, he waved up at them.

The crowd was cheering, roaring, whistling and chirping!

"I guess we did good!" exclaimed Zak.

"Yeah," answered Ivy, "who do you think won?"

Harmonia looked puzzled. "Won?"

"Yeah," said Zak, "who won the game?"

"Everybody won," said Orto. "If you play, you win."

"It's the playing and the sharing that count," added Harmonia.

The games went on. The children hopped like frogs. They swam like fish. They burrowed like groundhogs, and played Who Can Walk the Slowest. When the games were finished, the professor joined them and they all walked up to the nursery, ate some fruit, and headed back to the square.

They stopped to see the nest builders, the rock pilers, the cocoon weavers, the web spinners, the dam builders and the other craftlings.

And the sharing was extraordinary! One Shareling's head had become so swollen with ideas it had grown to twice its regular size. He was talking nonstop . . . solving problems and discussing ideas with anybody who would listen. The children watched in amazement as his head was slowly shrinking back to normal.

Another had a house on the square that had grown top-heavy with things she had accumulated over the years. It was tilting dangerously over to one side from the extra weight in the attic. She was furiously giving things away to everyone who walked by, and the house was slowly straightening itself out.

One incredibly fat Shareling was happily sharing food with all the people around. No wonder he was happy: right in front of their astonished eyes, he was growing thinner with every morsel he handed out. Zak and Ivy got a piece of delicious chocolate cake, and Ziggy was thrilled with the succulent biscuit the grateful Quantian handed him.

"Does everybody on Quantia share like this?" asked Zak. "Does everyone have to?"

"No one has to share," answered Angelicus, "but it makes

them feel good inside to share. After all, this is the day of balancing. The Great Universal Source gives everyone a special talent and gift in life. Like the bee sharing its honey, this is our chance to share a part of ourselves."

Suddenly a gasp spread through the crowd. Zak and Ivy looked up nervously to see what was causing the commotion. At the top of the square, flying low, came an astonishingly immense dragonfly. The fluttering of its four iridescent wings sent a low hum through the air. Its twenty-foot body hovered and darted above the booths and tents. It headed straight toward Angelicus and the children and settled down right in front of them. Ziggy leaped into Zak's arms at the sight of the insect's awesome face. The children jumped back.

The creature announced in a low buzz: "The Grand Council would like a word with you—with all of you."

"Professor," whispered Zak, "what did we do? Why do they want us?"

"What did you do?" Angelicus exploded with a delighted roar. "You helped me get home, that's what you did! They want to thank you."

"Odona!" yelled Orto.

He and Harmonia ran up and put their arms around the outlandish insect's long, thin body.

"Who's the dragonfly?" asked Ivy.

"That's Odona," said Angelicus. "She grew up on the family farm. But now she's working with the Grand Council."

"Hop aboard," buzzed Odona, "it's time for the Grand Parade."

"Parade?" said Zak.

"There's always a parade at the Rainbow Festival," said Angelicus gleefully, "and apparently we're leading it this time."

Ziggy barked and jumped out of Zak's arms. In his excitement, he forgot he could fly. Suddenly he was high in the air. But he quickly landed back on his feet. He loved parades!

The children, Ziggy, and Angelicus scrambled onto Odona's back.

"Harmonia, Orto," called Zak to their new friends, "aren't you coming with us?"

"Not on Odona," said Harmonia. "You and Uncle Aquius are going to meet with the Grand Council, so you ride at the head of the parade. We'll be right behind you."

The four giant fluted wings of the dragonfly began to spin. The crowd stepped back as the magnificent insect slowly rose like a helicopter into the air and headed toward the river. All the Sharelings gaily followed.

"Where is the Grand Council?" Zak asked.

"At the bottom of Great Spirit Mountain," said Angelicus. "The parade goes down the River of Tranquility to the Waterfall of Dreams. The Council Chambers are in a cavern behind the falls."

Odona skimmed along the surface of the sparkling river. Red, blue, and yellow canoes, rowboats and sailboats followed. They were filled to the brim with Quantians and Universal Sharelings. Some swam in the parade while others chose to fly. The silver creatures boomed like drums as they bounced on the river road and the green stick beings whistled as they floated through the air. Along the riverbank, Sharelings danced and marched, and turned somersaults and cartwheels like circus clowns. The trees and flowers pulled up their roots and walked along, singing "Love is the Hero, Here," the Quantian anthem.

"Wow," said Zak, looking back, "this really is something! Am I glad we came here!"

Ivy exclaimed, "No wonder you couldn't wait to get home for the Rainbow Festival, Professor!"

Ziggy wagged his tail. He was so happy to be in a parade!

THE GRAND COUNCIL AT GREAT SPIRIT MOUNTAIN

The two setting suns of Quantia lit the sky with an astonishing array of fiery colors. The parade moved down the river till it reached a sparkling lake at the base of the Waterfall of Dreams. Odona headed toward the falls and stopped before the cascading rainbow-colored water as the other paraders sat down in the grass on either side of the lake.

She hovered there for a moment. She clicked and she buzzed; then she announced loudly: "It is I, Odona, on official business for the Grand Council—requesting entry into the Chambers, please." Then she clicked and buzzed some more.

The wind blew down off of Great Spirit Mountain and the ringing of a hundred heavenly bells echoed through the sweet-smelling air. The Waterfall of Dreams swirled around and around. Then the cascading rainbow water began to flow backward up the white mountain, like a giant living theater curtain. The water rolled up and up till it disappeared high into the mist, and revealed a mystical cavern nestled deep in the base of Great Spirit Mountain.

Odona and her passengers glided through the arched entranceway, and the waterfall came roaring back down behind them, into the lake.

The walls of the cave were crystal-clear quartz and the floor was gold and silver. Floating in the air above their heads was what appeared to be a miniature universe, with twinkling galaxies and blazing suns. There were millions of tiny shining balls . . . blue, pink, orange, green, purple . . . every color imaginable.

At the end of the room five Quantians stood at a long sparkling crystal table.

"Professor," whispered Ivy, "is that the Grand Council?"

"That's them." Angelicus nodded his head.

Behind the Grand Council was a large mural of Great Spirit Mountain and the Waterfall of Dreams. Hundreds of figures were on the misty white mountain and they were all holding hands. There were Quantians, animals, humans and other beings and, unlike any picture the children had ever seen, the figures were disappearing and reappearing, moving in and out of the mist!

"Professor," whispered Zak, "what is that picture? Some of them look human!"

"I've seen some of them before—in books," said Ivy.

"That's the Living Mural of Eternity and those are all the Great Leaders of Kindness," answered the professor with a smile. "Beings that make a difference on their home planet. They're from the past, the present and the future, and they come from all the planets in the universe."

Odona approached the crystal table. A large medallion of gold, copper and silver was centered in its surface.

Zak remarked, "That's like the insignia on your belt, Professor."

"That's right," said Angelicus, "the Quantian Emblem of Interconnection."

Odona stopped and gracefully settled down onto the floor. The children, Angelicus, and Ziggy jumped from her back and walked up to the shimmering table. The room was very quiet. Zak and Ivy felt butterflies in their stomachs. Ziggy's tail twitched nervously, and he jumped into Zak's arms to get a better view.

The five members of the Grand Council stood solemnly. Each was a different color . . . black, red, yellow, brown and white, and they were all dressed in tunics woven of the finest golden silk threads. Like Angelicus, the Council members all had green ears and golden flower antennas. But their eyes weren't aquamarine— they were mirrors—shiny silver mirrors!

The Grand Council looked at the travelers. A warm, peaceful feeling came over the children and they could see reflections of the room in the eyes of the five Council members.

After a moment, the brown Quantian spoke: "Welcome home, Aquius Botanicus Angelicus. I see you have brought friends with you, from the Big Blue Ball."

"Yes, Shamash, I have," responded the professor. "I'd like you to meet Ivy, Zak, and Ziggy. They have been true Sharelings to me—Sharelings of the highest order. Without their help, I would have never found the pure water I needed to get home."

"Thank you so much, Zak, Ivy, and Ziggy, for bringing the professor home," said the Council member. "It's a pleasure to meet you. My name is Shamash."

Then he introduced the other four members of the Grand Council. The black Council member's name was Tara. The red one was called Pyros. Ethera was the name of the yellow member, and the white one was introduced as Luna. All five members of the Grand Council nodded their heads. Their flower antennas glowed.

"Welcome, Sharelings of the universe," they said, smiling. "Welcome to Quantia. Welcome to the Land of Sparkle."

"Pleased to meet you, too!" said the children.

Ziggy cocked his head and wagged his tail.

Shamash turned back to Angelicus. "And how are our brothers and sisters on Nega?"

The professor bowed his head as his eyes filled up with aquamarine tears. "I'm afraid I couldn't save Nega," he answered. "I did the best that I could do, but I only saved a few—a million or two. I was running very short on water, so I transported them to the nearest galaxy—to the little Pink Ball, Megador. The Megadoreans have very big hearts and they took every one of the refugees in."

"It breaks my heart to hear this news—that Nega is no more," said Shamash. A crystal-clear tear ran down his face.

Shamash came around the table and the other members of the Council followed. He stretched his right arm out, the palm of his hand facing Angelicus.

"But we thank you, Aquius, for doing the best that you could do. For giving all that you could give. We honor you for having served the Sharelings of the universe with great kindness."

"Thank you, my friend," said Angelicus, pressing his right palm to the open palm of Shamash.

The two Quantians bowed and touched foreheads. Their two flower antennas intertwined and they were surrounded by a soft, warm, glowing light. Ivy and Zak could see the love and compassion in Angelicus' eyes reflected in the mirror eyes of Shamash.

Then the rest of the Grand Council thanked the professor in turn. Pyros, the red Shareling, said that it took great courage and faith to go to Nega and do what he had to do. Black-skinned Tara commended him for understanding the plight of the Negans and she thanked him for the wisdom he showed in the rescue. Ethera praised him for his willingness to give and for sharing the last of his water. With a soft smile on her white face, Luna told Angelicus she knew that the painful loss of Nega must have been a very dark moment for him. But in his accepting and facing the truth, it would only reflect light back onto the rest of the universe. She applauded him for his commitment to truth and honesty.

After each greeting, the Council members and Angelicus looked into each other's eyes, touched palms and foreheads, and their antennas intertwined. Zak and Ivy could see the emotions the Quantians were sharing. They could feel these feelings in their own hearts.

When the Council was finished honoring the professor, Shamash turned to the children and Ziggy. "Now. Zak, Ivy, and Ziggy," said Shamash, "how are things on your Big Blue Ball?"

"Well, sir," said Zak shyly, "I'm afraid things are a little out of balance there, too."

"The water could be cleaner," added Ivy.

Ziggy barked. He agreed with his friends. Things could be a lot better back home.

CHAPTER SEVENTEEN

The Council members nodded compassionately.

"Mmm," said Shamash, "we understand. But you've become a part of us now. You have given to us all by helping the professor. So if you ever need us to give to you or if you ever need our help on the Big Blue Ball, we want you to feel free to call on us here at Great Spirit Mountain. In light of that, we'd like to entrust all of you with the keys you will need for your return."

Three shimmering figures floated down out of the mural on the wall and came toward the table! Two of the figures were human in shape and about the size of Zak and Ivy. The light surrounding them was so intense the astonished children couldn't even make out their faces. Each of the mysterious, luminescent figures carried a white silken pillow in its outstretched arms. The third figure was a four-legged animal and had a pair of wings. It was about the size of Ziggy and bore a pillow on its back. It looked like a flying dog!

Ivy whispered, "Who are they, Professor?"

"Why, they visit your Big Blue Ball from time to time. I think you call them Angels," answered the professor. "They're from the Great White Ball."

Floating just above the floor, the figures joined the Grand Council. On one of the pillows was a pipe just like the professor's, with three feathers hanging from the bowl. On the next was a bubble-blowing wand. On the back of the flying dog, the pillow held a small rainbow collar with a sparkling medallion of the Quantian Emblem of Interconnection.

"If you would be so kind as to step forward," said Shamash.

The children stepped up to the Council and Ziggy jumped from Zak's arms.

"Ziggy," Shamash said, "as the representative of Love and

Compassion, and speaking for the rest of the Grand Council who represent Courage and Faith, Wisdom and Understanding, Truth and Honesty and Giving and Sharing, as well as for all Great Leaders of Kindness, past, present and future, I thank you."

The angelic dog floated forward and Shamash reached down to take the collar from the pillow. The light around the creature dimmed a little and its face came into focus.

"Zak," Ivy gasped, "the Angel looks just like Ziggy!"

Shamash knelt down and fastened the collar around Ziggy's neck.

"We honor you, Ziggy of the Big Blue Ball," he said, "for having shown the five great qualities of a true Shareling. And, most of all, for doing the best that you can do. We are pleased to present you this, our highest honor: the Emblem of Interconnection."

Shamash touched Ziggy's forehead and Ziggy kissed Shamash on the nose. The medallion on his collar thundered and let out a brilliant flash of light. Ziggy jumped back, but when he realized it was his collar that made the noise, he straightened up to his full height and proudly strutted back to stand next to Zak and Ivy. He felt as big as a Great Dane.

Shamash stood up. The other pillow bearers came forward and floated on either side of him, smiling. Zak and Ivy could see that they were duplicates of themselves.

"And now," said Shamash, "Zak and Ivy of the Big Blue Ball. For doing the best that you can do, the Grand Council of Quantia takes great pleasure in honoring you with our highest award.

"The wand and the pipe are the two most precious tools of the Quantian civilization. They were given to us by the Great Universal Source. Whenever you dip your wand or pipe into the sparkle, you will have the ability to travel through all times and dimensions. These tools give you the power to heal, to protect, to share and to communicate with all Sharelings in the universe. May you always use them with great compassion, courage, wisdom, honesty, and with a totally giving heart."

Shamash took the white wand from the silk pillow and presented it to Ivy. The handle was covered with little buttons and lights, just like the stem of the professor's pipe.

"Thank you, Shamash," she said. "This is the best gift in the whole world!"

With love in his eyes, the brown Quantian cradled Ivy's face in his hands and touched his forehead to hers. As their eyes met, the sound of a great wind filled the air. The wand shimmered and vibrated in Ivy's hands and instantly the thin handle turned into the grip of a sword! A brilliant flash of white light shot out of the sword handle. It shot right through Pyros, lighting up the red Quantian's big, beating heart like an x-ray, and clear across the room into the crystal wall. Then, as quickly as it had appeared, the sword of light turned back into the white wand.

"Gee, Shamash," said Ivy, wide eyed, "what just happened?"

"That, my young friend, was the sword of white light. The sword of doing good," he answered. "Just push the white button on your wand, and you will see into the hearts of all Sharelings. It helps blow away evil and fill up the dark places of confusion and anger with the light of love. You are now a Peaceful Warrior."

Shamash picked up the pipe and presented it to Zak. He put his hand on Zak's head, looked deep into his eyes, and their foreheads met. Zak felt touched by a feeling—a feeling of love down deep in his core.

"Thanks a million, Shamash," he said, overwhelmed. "This is an extremely excellent gift!"

The Quantian smiled back at him. "Why don't you try pushing the rainbow button, Zak?" he said playfully.

Zak did as he suggested and his hand started tingling where he held the pipe. The buttons flashed up and down the stem and then with a pop and a roar, the pipe transformed into a sword of sparkling multicolored light! It gurgled and shot out a swirling, rippling rainbow and joined everyone in the Grand Council Chambers together in one big rainbow-colored bubble. Everyone in the room was glowing and sharing a wonderful feeling! They could feel everything in each other's hearts and souls. The effect only lasted for a second, then the sword turned back into a pipe.

"Oh, wow! It felt like we were all one person!" exclaimed Zak.

"As you can see," said Shamash, "yours is a sword as well, Zak—the sword of rainbow light—the sword of unity and oneness of spirit. It can help you do good by bringing Sharelings together. By helping them see that deep down in our core we're really all made of the same stuff. Your sword can help shake loose misunderstanding and illuminate the Great Truth that lies beneath all things. You, Zak, are now a Warrior of the Rainbow."

Shamash stepped back to stand with the rest of the Grand Council. The Angels floated up into the air and rejoined the other Great Leaders of Kindness in the mural. Then the five Quantians bowed and returned to their places at the table.

Professor Angelicus looked proudly at the children and Ziggy.

"This has been a wonderful day for every Shareling in the universe," he said. "Now it's time for us to join the others. We don't want to miss the Closing Ceremonies of the Rainbow Festival. It's a spectacular sky show."

Odona had been patiently standing by, waiting for her passengers. Now the travelers, carefully holding their new treasures, mounted the dragonfly.

"Farewell, gentle Sharelings. Thank you for coming," said Shamash. "Until we meet again, travel in peace."

"Goodbye," answered the star-struck children, "thanks for everything. This has been totally awesome!"

Ziggy wagged his tail, his eyes sparkling as he barked "Goodbye!"

Odona clicked and buzzed and the rainbow Waterfall of Dreams rolled up the mountain again and let the party through. Night had fallen on the Land of Sparkle while they were inside meeting with the Grand Council. The Quantian sky was filled with a million twinkling stars and four full yellow moons. The stars were like sequins; they each glittered a different color.

Odona scooted across the lake and landed near Harmonia and Orto. The professor, Ziggy, and the children said goodbye to Odona and ran over to join them. They all sat down to wait for the great sky show to begin.

Almost immediately, streaks of lightning zigzagged in all directions across the Quantian sky and the heavens began to thunder and roar. The ground shook beneath the grass, and Ziggy jumped into Zak's lap, shivering.

The professor saw him and gently said, "Don't worry, Ziggy. It's not going to rain. That lightning will stay in the sky. The sky Sharelings have been saving up their best energy for a billion years and now they're sharing it with all of us."

Oohs and aahs rose up from the crowd as millions of vivid colors were created by the electrical energy flashing from cloud to cloud.

Zak yelled over the awesome noise, "Professor, this is great! I never knew lightning could be this beautiful!"

"Oh, that's nothing," said Orto. "Here come the shooting stars!"

Far up, near each of the Quantian moons, small clusters of twinkling, multicolored stars flashed into the four corners of the sky. They streaked toward Great Spirit Mountain, leaving long glittering trails of sparkling, fiery stardust behind them. Down they came, disappearing into the mist of the giant mountain, and then shooting out again in perfect formation. The rainbow-colored star clusters zoomed around and around the mountain, coming closer and closer to the spectators. Just as it seemed they would hit the lake, the brilliantly blazing meteorites rocketed upward. They looped and swooped as they headed back into the stratosphere, and a great sigh went up from the Sharelings as a million bits of glittering, golden stardust sprinkled down onto the meadow. The crowd was going crazy!

The great sky show celebration came to a grand finale as ribbons and sheets of shimmering auroras lit the heavens and a gigantic lightning bolt arced from horizon to horizon across the Quantian sky. The lightning struck the rainbow Waterfall of Dreams with an awesome roar and brilliantly lit up the flowing water. The bells of the ringing rocks chimed; and, as giant bubbles rose up from the waterfall, the spectators cheered and applauded. Swirling, glittering and sparkling, the bubbles slowly floated out over the countryside.

A voice reverberated across the lake: "And that's all, folks. Another rainbow celebration comes to a spectacular end. We hope we see you all back here in another billion years!"

The Sharelings got up and stretched, and started heading back toward the village. They were passing the nursery when the professor's pipe spoke up.

"Prepare for departure. Prepare for departure," it called. "The Purple Ball needs you."

The professor laughed. "Oh, I was having so much fun, I almost forgot! I have an important appointment on the Purple Ball and I've got to get going."

"Professor," said Ivy, worried, "aren't you taking us home?"

"Me?" He smiled. "You don't need me. You have the tools to get home now. We're leaving from the same gate, though. So of course I'll see you off. But I'm running late, so we'd better hurry. We should fly."

Ivy, Zak, and Ziggy turned to Harmonia and Orto.

"Well," said Ivy, "I guess this is goodbye."

"You'll be coming back, won't you?" asked Orto.

"You've got to come back and visit our farm," said Harmonia.

"I'd love to," said Ivy.

Zak looked back at the mist over the mountain. "I want to come back. I want to climb Great Spirit Mountain," he said.

Zak and Ivy hugged Harmonia and Orto. Ziggy kissed the two Quantians on the nose.

"OK, kids, focus on flying," said Angelicus.

They all rose into the air and flew over the little village, over Karmapa, alongside the Rainbow Bridge, through the heart-shaped golden gate, and landed on the soft, velvety green grass.

RETURN TO THE RIVER

Professor Angelicus held out a small crystal bottle like the one he carried in his belt.

"Here is a bottle of water from the Waterfall of Dreams," he said. "It will fuel your pipe and your wand so you can come visit me whenever you like."

"Oh, Professor," sighed Ivy, "we're gonna miss you so much!" She hugged Angelicus.

"Yeah, Professor," said Zak, "we'll always be friends, won't we?"

"Absolutely, Zak," said Angelicus softly, putting his arm around the boy.

Ivy and Zak had tears in their eyes. Ziggy whimpered and jumped into the professor's arms, furiously licking his green ears. Ziggy didn't want to leave; he wouldn't be able to fly when he got back to Earth.

"Professor, how can we get in touch with you?" asked Zak.

"When you need me, you'll remember. Just look into the sparkle anywhere and concentrate real hard. Remember Bubble Time, and remember—the sparkle is the window to Quantia. Just call—I'll be there in a jiffy."

The professor smiled lovingly at his three friends.

"Well," he said, "the three of you have certainly been a light in my life, and I will miss you. But I've got to get going. And anyway, Zak, you've got to get home for dinner. You don't want to be late!"

The children laughed.

Zak glanced at his watch and his expression turned serious. "But, Professor, how *do* we do it?" he asked. "How do we get home?"

"You know how to get home, Zak," said Angelicus. "Be true to yourself and follow your starpath. Your body and mind will take you. Your heart will lead you. Your spirit remembers!"

He chuckled. "But you're not going anywhere without a bubble, Zak. Pour a little water in the end of Ivy's wand."

Zak opened the crystal bottle and poured a few drops into Ivy's bubble wand. Lights blinked up and down the handle and the wand began to glow. Soon an iridescent sheet of water filled the hoop.

"It's ready, Professor," Ivy said. "What do I do now?"

"Why, make a bubble," he said, laughing. "You can blow one or you can stick out your wand and let the wind help you."

Ivy held out the wand and ran around in a circle. The air flowed through the hoop and quickly enclosed them all in a shining, shimmering bubble.

The professor laughed again. "I'm not going with you!" he exclaimed as the bubble rose a little into the air. He pushed through the skin of the bubble and jumped down onto the grass.

Ziggy looked like he was going to jump out after him but his rag rug had appeared on the invisible floor of the bubble, along with Zak and Ivy's chairs. So he dug a hole in the rug, curled up and got ready for takeoff.

They waved goodbye to the professor. Ivy pushed the red button on the wand and a female voice called out: "Destination, Big Blue Ball."

A galactic breeze blew down from the twinkling stars of the Quantian sky and the bubble began to spin. It spun ten times to the right and then ten times to the left. Faster and faster it spun and swiftly swirled into outer space. A white highway of light appeared in front of them.

"There it is, Ivy," said Zak. "There's the road that'll take us home. There's our starpath."

Ziggy stood up and wagged his tail.

The bubble rolled onto the road of light. It rolled and rolled, faster and faster. Faster than the speed of light! And in less than an instant, with one gigantic flash, the children and the little dog could see the Earth.

"Look, Ivy," whispered Zak, "look at our Big Blue Ball."

Ivy sighed, "Look how beautiful it is!"

"Yeah," said Zak, "I can't wait to get home."

"Me too," said Ivy.

Ziggy barked excitedly.

The bubble spun down into the Earth's atmosphere. They sailed through miles and miles of white fluffy clouds, then finally came out high over the river. The sun was rising in the east. A gaggle of geese flew south. A farmer's field was overflowing with giant pumpkins and the leaves on the trees were orange, yellow and fiery red. They reflected brilliantly in the water below.

"Look, Zak, it's autumn. Remember when we collected leaves?" said Ivy.

"Yeah," Zak sighed, "it seems like a million years ago!" He glanced at his watch. The hands were spinning. "We're still in Bubble Time," he said. "We've traveled through all the seasons."

The leaves were falling off the trees as the bubble glided downstream. A school of slippery black and silver eels were swimming south, on their way to the ocean.

The voyagers flew over a row of abandoned houses along the riverbank. An osprey swooped by with a fish in its mouth and landed on a rooftop.

"Zak," said Ivy, "no one's living in those houses."

"My dad told me about that," said Zak. "They made all the people move out. They want to build a dam on the river and make a big lake."

"We can't let that happen," said Ivy. "The river won't like that. The river's got to flow—for all the Sharelings! One day, we'll be in charge. We'll be the Guardian Residents and we'll take care of the water."

Zak looked down at the river. "We've got the pipe and we've got the wand, Ivy," he said.

Ziggy barked and ran to the transparent wall of the bubble.

"Look," yelled Ivy, "there's your house!"

Zak saw his little stone house on the hill. The cornfields had been harvested and the husks were stacked high. He saw the creek and the gristmill and two turkey buzzards perched on top of the old gray barn, and the willow weeping out over the river.

A lone crow called out from the top of a giant ash. "Welcome back to Earth," it cawed.

The lights started blinking up and down the wand. It called out: "Prepare for landing. It's a beautiful day on the Big Blue Ball."

A huge gust of wind blasted down off the palisades. There was a crackling in the trees and the bubble spun around and around, swirling and twirling toward the riverbank, through the autumn leaves. With a thunderous roar and a brilliant burst of light, the bubble hit the ground and popped.

"Zak! Zak! Get up! Are you all right? You've got a bump on your head."

Ivy was shaking Zak on the shoulder and Ziggy was licking his forehead. Zak brought his hand to his forehead and felt a big bump just above his left eye.

Faint images—a misty white mountain—a crystal cave— huge aquamarine eyes—flashed through his mind. He blinked his eyes several times and looked at the branch lying over his knapsack and fishing rod. He was covered with twigs.

"Ivy, did the bubble pop?" he asked groggily. "I've got to get home for dinner!"

She laughed. "Dinner? It's still morning. Are you all right? I think that branch over there knocked you silly. We didn't even blow any bubbles yet!" She cocked her head quizzically. "How did you know I brought bubbles? My grandma just gave them to me! Are you OK?"

Zak pulled himself up. "Ah, it's just a little bump on the head," he said, and looked at his watch. He saw she was right; it was still morning.

"Then look," she said, "there's a pipe and a wand—and

they're magic! It says it right here on the bottle."

"Excellent!" said Zak.

"Here. You take the pipe and I'll take the wand."

They dipped the toys into the bottle and soon their bubbles were floating out over the river. Zak looked up. The sun was warm on his face. His eyes followed a rainbow bubble as it drifted high into the air. A feather fell from the sky and he ran to catch it before it hit the ground.

"Look, Ivy," he said, "an eagle feather!"

"But where's the eagle?" she asked.

"He's there, even if we can't see him," said Zak. "Wouldn't it be great if we could go inside a bubble and float—as high as an eagle? We could see the whole world! Maybe even go into outer space!"

Ivy laughed. "Oh, Zak, you're such a dreamer!"

Ziggy barked, ran up and jumped into Zak's arms. He wagged his tail and licked the bubble pipe. The medallion on his rainbow-colored collar was sparkling in the sun.

MumbleFish Books